NOT ANOTHER FAKE MARRIAGE

Not Another Romance Novel

R.L. KENDERSON

Not Another Fake Marriage

Chapter One

ALEXIS

"PAISLEY, I'm so happy for you," I said to one of my closest friends. "I'm sorry I was so cynical about Colin."

Paisley had recently begun dating, and when it'd started to get serious, I hadn't been the most supportive. Probably because of my own failed marriage. But at least I recognized that and was able to apologize.

"It's okay. I know your heart was in the right place." She picked up her menu.

It was my monthly dinner with my friends from high school. We'd all met in choir and stayed close, even after all the years we'd been out of school.

A few months ago, we had decided to turn our monthly dinners into a club because we'd all been single and sick of men. We'd even come up with the most ridiculous name—United She-Woman Single Ladies with Our Vibrators So We Never Have Another Bad Date or Experience Romance Again Because Men Suck Club—but it always made me smile. However, the hate was running low with my friends, seeing as one was married, one was engaged, one was seeing someone, and one was starting a new relationship. But I still was nowhere near ready to date again.

"So, what is everyone having?" Paisley asked.

"Oh my God," Tessa said.

"Oh shit," Bree said.

Paisley jerked her head up to see what our friends were looking at, and I could already tell by the look on her face that it wasn't good.

"Alexis," she warned, but by now, I was turning in my seat to see what Tessa and Bree were talking about.

As soon as my eyes landed on what they were all freaking out about, the blood drained from my face.

It was my ex-husband with another woman. She was young and pregnant.

A rock formed in my stomach.

"That motherfucker," Pru hissed. "He won't give you the money for your half of the house, and now, we know why."

Kevin was supposed to sell the house we'd bought when we got married and then give me half the proceeds. It was in our divorce decree, but he'd been putting it off, knowing I couldn't afford to take him to court again. Meanwhile, I'd been living in a small apartment, trying to save money for the café and bakery Tessa and I had just opened.

I was pinching pennies, and he was living happily with a new woman.

The lady shifted, and I caught a better look at her face.

I spun back around to my friends. "I think I'm going to be sick. That woman—" I covered my mouth. I couldn't say the words out loud.

"Honey, we saw," Bree said. "She's pregnant."

"And by the looks of that belly, she was pregnant before they were divorced," Pru said, crossing her arms and shaking her head.

"It's not that. I mean, it is, but..." I said.

My ex and I had tried for several years to have a baby, but we'd been unsuccessful. While I was now glad since I didn't have to co-parent with Kevin, it hurt to see he was getting something I wanted very badly. It made me feel like I was half a woman.

"What?" Paisley asked gently.

"That's Candace," I said.

My friends exchanged glances, but they had blank looks on their faces.

"Who's Candace?" Paisley asked.

Thankfully, before I had to answer, Tessa gasped. "Oh my God, Candace? She was your exchange student."

The last year of our marriage, we'd opened a home to an exchange student since we still hadn't gotten pregnant.

It seemed that while I had been baking to ease the pain of an unhappy marriage, Kevin had been fucking the young woman and knocking her up. We'd been married for four years but together since college, and it had come down to this.

I nodded to confirm Tessa was right, and someone gasped.

Pru slammed her fist against the table. "Let's turn him in."

God, I wish.

"She was nineteen when she came to live with us. She's probably twenty now." I shook my head in defeat. *It isn't fair.*

"Dammit," Pru said.

"Are you going to be okay?" Paisley asked me.

I pushed my chair back and stood up. "I need a minute."

"Do you want one of us to come with you?" Tessa asked.

Shaking my head, I said, "No. I'll be right back."

I made my way to the back of the restaurant, where the restrooms were, and went inside the ladies' room. I started to pace back and forth in front of the sink.

It didn't really surprise me that my ex was with someone now, but I was shocked with whom. Her parents had trusted us to take care of her, and Kevin had preyed on her. And I didn't know if I was any better since it seemed to have happened under my nose.

I slapped a hand over my mouth as bile rose in my throat. I spun around and went into a stall. Waiting, I counted the seconds until my stomach settled before I walked out again.

But just as I was exiting my stall, the door opened, and Candace came in. We both froze, and my eyes traveled down to her protruding belly.

I was hit with so many thoughts at once.

My ex was not the perfect man and left a lot to be desired, but I'd never thought he was the kind of guy to sleep with someone so young, especially someone like our exchange student. I didn't understand how I'd judged someone so poorly and how I had been married to him.

It was apparent that all those fertility tests I'd done were for nothing. My doctor had told me that they couldn't find anything wrong, and since Kevin had refused to get tested, I had assumed it was him. The big pregnant abdomen staring at me said my physician had been wrong. It was me.

I couldn't be there a moment longer to process the rest of my thoughts.

"Excuse me," I said, stepping around Candace.

"Please, let me explain," she said.

I glared at her. "I don't want to hear any of your excuses. I brought you into my home and cared for you.

Not once did you say a word to me about sleeping with my then husband, much less having his baby."

"It's not what you think. Please, Alexis."

I looked down and scoffed. "Oh, but I think it is. If you know what's good for you, you'll get away from him before it's too late."

Quickly, I left before she could say another word to me because part of me empathized with her. I, too, had been enchanted by Kevin's charm at one time. But I couldn't be around Candace. I knew it wouldn't be good for my mental health.

When I got back to the table, Tessa asked, "Are you going to be all right?"

"As soon as I figure out how to get my money from Kevin, I will be." I couldn't fix the past, but I could at least get what he owed me. "I'm sick of that asshole jerking me around." I looked up at my friends, determination flooding me. "I know our little club is mostly a fun joke, but I'm so grateful for it and the six of you because I am *never* getting married again. That bastard has ruined me forever."

Chapter Two

TREVOR

"HELLO, NANA." I gave my grandmother a kiss on her cheek and took my usual seat next to her at her dining room table.

She put her hand on top of mine. "Hello, dear."

I studied her. I knew my grandma loved me. Without any hesitation, she and my grandfather had taken in my brother and me after our parents died in a car accident, but she didn't always hand out affection.

"Are you doing okay, Nana?"

"Yes. Of course," she said as she slipped her hand away from mine without making eye contact with me. Something was definitely going on with her, but before I could pry, she asked, "Where do you think your brother is?"

I snorted. "Who cares?"

"*Trevor*," she scolded me.

"Sorry. But honestly, I have no idea."

7

What Kevin wanted, Kevin did. He didn't care about anyone else, including our grandparents. When our grandfather had passed away last year, he had come late to the funeral.

Five minutes later, the front door opened.

"I'm here," Kevin shouted.

"Wonderful," Nana said. My brother walked into the dining room, and she smiled at him. "I'm so glad you could make it."

"I wouldn't have missed it, Nana." Kevin looked at me. "Hey, Trevor."

"Hey."

"Sit down, Kevin," Nana said. "And start dishing up."

I picked up the mashed potatoes in front of me. My Nana made the best mashed potatoes. After putting two large spoonfuls on my plate, I turned to her. "Do you want some?"

"Yes, please, but only a little."

I frowned in concern. This didn't seem like her, but I scooped up some potatoes for her and put them on her plate. "Kevin?"

My brother took the bowl from my hand as he shoved the plate of meatloaf at our grandmother.

"Nana, do you want me to help you with that?" I asked her in a tone directed toward my brother to hint that he was unhelpful.

"Trevor, I'm old, not incapable."

Kevin smirked at me.

I ignored him and finished packing my plate with my grandmother's home cooking.

As Kevin and I stuffed our mouths, Nana picked at her food. When she caught me looking, she shoved a bite in her mouth.

Kevin and I didn't meet up for dinner at her home very often, so I'd had a feeling she wanted to talk about something important. But seeing her now, I was sure of it. What had her so nervous that she couldn't even eat was the big question though.

Because she was obviously anxious, I didn't press her about anything. But as we neared the end of our meal, only making small talk, I began to worry it was something serious and Nana wasn't going to say it.

"Nana, I have someone I'd like you to meet," Kevin said.

"Oh. Have you started dating again?"

He smiled. "Something like that."

"I'm happy for you. You deserve a nice woman."

My brother had already had a nice woman, but he'd thrown his ex-wife, Alexis, away like she was nothing. Last I'd heard, he still owed her money.

And my poor grandmother had no idea how Kevin had treated his ex, and if she wasn't so elderly, I would let her know. But she didn't have that many years left, and I figured it was nicer to keep her in bliss before she passed than to live with being disappointed in someone she'd helped raise.

Nana turned to me. "What about you, Trevor? Anyone new in your life?"

I shook my head. "Not since Lorraine."

"That was two years ago."

"It was?" I quickly did the math in my head. "I guess you're right." I shrugged.

"Trevor, I wish you'd find someone."

I smiled. "Nana, why are you asking me this? You never bother me about my dating life."

With a sigh, my grandmother sat back in her chair, looking defeated.

"Nana?" I said.

I looked at Kevin. Even he seemed concerned.

"Boys, I need to tell you something."

Uh-oh.

"I went to the doctor today, a specialist. He told me I have ovarian cancer. It's stage four."

The food in my throat felt like a lump of nothing, and I forced it down. "What does that mean?" I asked.

"It means, I likely have only a month or two to live."

My heart sank into my stomach. I wasn't ready to lose her.

———

I twirled the alcohol in my glass and took a long drink before I went to find my brother.

He was in our grandfather's study.

"Where's Nana?" he asked.

"I left her in the family room." I closed the door. "You and I need to talk."

"About what?"

"You know what."

"You mean, the pharmacy?" Kevin asked as he sat behind the large mahogany desk.

"Yes," I said as I reluctantly took one of the two chairs across from him.

My grandparents had both been pharmacists, and in the '60s, they'd opened their own independent pharmacy in their small town. They'd only had one child—our father, who passed away when we were kids, leaving my brother and me to inherit the business.

"We need to figure out what's going to happen when the will goes into effect," I said.

Our father had also been a pharmacist and the one who was supposed to take over Nelson Pharmacy when my grandparents retired, but that plan had ended the minute my father died. My grandfather had told Kevin and me our whole lives that it was our job to grow up and run it one day, but that hadn't happened.

Kevin never had any intention of following in our family's footsteps. He'd left our small town the day after he graduated, only coming home to visit about once a year for the first five years he was gone. Not that I really blamed him.

I had tried the pharmacy thing. I went to college and worked hard to get into the program, but it wasn't for me. I had no interest in the profession, and I had no desire to live in the small town I had grown up in either. I broke it to my grandparents that I was switching my major to land surveying. It was what I had really wanted to do since high school after working for a land surveying company. Nana was disappointed, but she understood. Our grandfather was furious.

He was so mad that in his will, he wrote that to inherit the business, Kevin and I either had to become pharmacists or be married. Apparently, he'd felt this was his only way of making us show a serious commitment to something. If neither of us fulfilled his expectations, the pharmacy would go to some third cousin, twice removed, we'd never met and who probably didn't even know about the will.

But that had been twenty years ago. We, including my grandmother, thought it had been a joke or a temporary will that he would exchange for a new one once he got over his anger. But when he'd died last year, we'd all found out the will was real. He had left my grandmother in charge until one of us *came to our senses*. And because the business had opened in the '60s, my grandmother's name wasn't on any of the paperwork. She didn't own a dime of that place. I guessed we were lucky my grandfather had made sure she would get the house and was taken care of. The old bastard had loved his wife, but he had been sexist as hell.

So, now, here we were, both without pharmacy degrees or wives.

I didn't want to be a pharmacist, but I didn't want my grandparents' business to go to some stranger either.

"I can contact Grandpa's lawyer and see if he can give us any advice," I told Kevin. "And once that's figured out, since you and I both live less than an hour away, we can take turns looking after things. The store has great employees, so it should be fairly easy."

"There's no need." A smile spread across my brother's face.

"There's no need for what? To take turns?"

"To contact Grandpa's attorney."

"How can you say that? Nana will be devastated if something happens to that place."

Kevin leaned forward. "Nana will be dead and won't know what happens to it. Besides, I'm getting married next week."

"First of all, you're a callous asshole. And two, *what*? To who?"

Who in their right mind would want to marry my brother after the way he treated his first wife?

Kevin picked up his phone, made a few swipes, and handed it to me.

"What the fuck? Is that who I think it is?"

"Yes. She had to go back to Canada for a while. It took a bit to get her back in the States on a visa, but we were able to do so a few weeks ago."

"And that's your baby?" Before my brother could answer, I set his phone on the desk and stopped any response he was about to give me with my hand. "You know what? I don't want to know. She's so young."

"She's twenty. And you don't know the whole story."

"I don't care what the whole story is."

He was almost thirty-five. I felt sorry for the poor girl. And for Alexis. I wondered if she had any clue who Kevin was with now.

"Regardless if you care or not, in a few weeks, she'll be my wife. I was going to marry her anyway, but in light of Nana's news, this is working out better than I thought it would."

It was an odd choice of words to talk about his future wife, but it was a relief to know that we wouldn't have to worry about the pharmacy.

I stood. "Let's concentrate on getting Nana through this diagnosis for now. But when the time comes, let me know if you need any help with the pharmacy."

"Thanks, but I won't."

He seemed pretty confident.

"Okay. I'm glad you got it all figured out."

He shrugged. "It wasn't hard. I'm going to sell it."

I waited for Kevin to tell me he was joking.

"Remember that developer who was sniffing around a few months back? I'm sure he's still interested in the land."

"*You can't sell the pharmacy and have it torn down,*" I practically shouted. "It's our legacy. Our grandparents started that place. Our mom and dad met there. And so many people in this town count on it for work and health care."

"I'm sorry, but they're going to have to look elsewhere."

"How can you be so heartless?"

"It's business. Small, independent pharmacies don't make as much as they used to with the changes insurance companies have put into place. Nelson Pharmacy hasn't been able to compete with the big chains for a long time."

I sighed. In my head, I knew he was right, but in my heart, it felt wrong. "I know that, but you can't just sell it and let someone demolish the place."

"Sure I can. I will give the employees plenty of notice to find other jobs."

I ran my hand through my hair. I couldn't let my brother do this. Unfortunately, I didn't have time to go to pharmacy school. I needed to figure something out.

Until then, I needed to stall my brother. If my grandmother knew, it would break her heart.

"Don't say anything to Nana."

Kevin scoffed, as if I'd dealt him the biggest insult. "I would never do that."

Right. But you'll sell the pharmacy and let someone tear it down the minute she's in the ground.

I left my grandfather's office before I wasted another breath, trying to convince my brother what he wanted to do was wrong.

Nana was sitting in the family room, where I'd left her.

"Is everything okay?" she asked as I sat next to her.

I smiled as well as I could. "It's fine, Nana." I was going to do my best to make sure it was anyway.

Chapter Three

ALEXIS

THE BELL over the door to The Purrfect Café & Bakery rang, and I glanced that way for a second before returning to my task. I immediately looked back, but I must have imagined him.

"What's wrong?" Tessa asked as she continued to stock the display case with the pastries I'd just brought out to her.

"I thought I saw my ex-brother-in-law, but I think my eyes were playing tricks on me."

I didn't want to tell her, but ever since I had seen Kevin and Candace, I hadn't been able to stop thinking about him. Not because I wanted him back. That was never happening again.

No, it was because I was jealous. Not of Candace, but of my ex. I'd always imagined that I would have a beautiful family. With the man I loved and our one or two kids running around. But instead, I was alone and childless, and unless I decided to adopt, it looked like I was staying that way. It wasn't fair that my asshole of an ex-husband had gotten the house, the partner, and a kid.

Even though I'd said I was never getting married again, it still hurt.

I didn't even have a pet to call my own because my apartment was so small. I didn't think it was fair. I knew life wasn't fair, but in this instance, it should have been. The bad guy wasn't supposed to win at the end of the movie.

"Oh, Trevor? When's the last time you saw him?"

"Oh jeez. Probably a month or two before I left Kevin, so it's been a while."

"Maybe he heard about our place and came to check it out."

"Maybe." I doubted it though. Who would have told him? Kevin? I didn't think so.

What I did think was that I needed to stop dwelling on what my ex was doing and focus on what I had. A new business. And someday, I would no longer be living in a shoebox.

"The ladies and I have been talking," Tessa said.

"Oh? About what?"

"You."

"You've been talking behind my back?" I joked.

She grinned. "Is it behind your back if I tell you about it later?"

"Yes."

She laughed.

"What was the conversation about?"

Tessa's face got serious. "We think you should make a GoFundMe to get enough money to hire a lawyer and get the money Kevin owes you."

For a second, I let myself consider it, but I quickly shook it away. "I can't do that."

"Why? You said yourself you were going to do everything you could to get the money he owes you."

"That was when I was mad and full of fire. But it doesn't change my situation. By the time I got the money, it would probably all go to an attorney anyway."

"Which is why you start a GoFundMe."

"It's my mess, Tessa. I can't let others pay for it or take charity."

She looked at me skeptically. "Oh, really? But you could meet my husband behind my back and let him fund our café?"

I laughed. "He wasn't your husband yet. And he's a silent partner. Not the same thing."

"Then, let Seth be a silent partner in getting your money back from Kevin."

"Nice try."

Tessa's husband owned a very profitable advertising agency and could definitely afford to pay for my lawyer, but I wasn't going to ask him to do that.

"Okay, then let me."

"No."

"You have to do something," she said.

"I think I might be able to help with that," a deep voice said.

We both turned to see Trevor standing at our counter.

My mouth dropped open. He was really here, and he looked amazing.

He was two years younger than Kevin, but he looked at least five. Not that Trevor looked young. Kevin just looked old.

Trevor had thick, dark hair, a beard to match, and deep brown eyes. I'd forgotten how handsome he was.

Truth be told, it was Trevor I had liked first when I met the brothers. But it was Kevin who had made the first and only move, so he was the one I'd ended up dating. If only I could go back and say no.

"How can you help her?" Tessa asked, her voice full of suspicion.

"If you don't mind, I'd like to talk to Alexis about that. Alone."

"Um, sure. Why don't you come in the back with me? I need to check the timer on the oven anyway."

Trevor followed me back into the kitchen just as the timer beeped. I inspected the cupcakes and took them out of the oven.

"I have to admit, I'm pretty curious as to what you can do to help me." And why he was even in my café in the first place.

"Technically, I said I think I might be able to help with that."

I sighed. "You're as bad as your brother."

Trevor straightened. "I absolutely am not."

He was obviously offended, and I held up a hand.

"I apologize. I didn't really mean it. Kevin would often claim that he didn't say something. That I misunderstood or I got a few words wrong."

"So, he gaslit you?" Trevor shook his head. "What an asshole," he muttered.

"Yeah. That's the word for it." I faced the cupcakes and fiddled with them, so he couldn't see my cheeks turn red. I was both embarrassed that I had let someone treat me like that and validated that he had put into words what Kevin had done to me. When I could no longer stall, I turned back. "Anyway, how do you think you might be able to help?"

Trevor looked down. "My grandmother is dying."

I gasped. "Oh no." I had always liked Nana Nelson, even at the end, when she no longer came around. I was sure that Kevin had filled her head with stories about me, and I didn't blame her. Kevin was her grandson. "What's wrong?"

Trevor cleared his throat and lifted his eyes. "Cancer. Stage Four."

"I'm so sorry."

"Thanks."

"If there's anything I can do..."

"There is something."

This was a surprise. "Oh?"

"Did Kevin ever tell you about my grandfather's will and how we needed to either be married or become a pharmacist to inherit the family business?"

"*That was true?*" I laughed at the ridiculousness of it. "I always thought he'd made it up."

"It seems like something he would do, but no, it's true. My grandfather was a spiteful bastard."

"I'll say. But what does this have to do with me?"

Trevor looked away. "I don't know how to tell you this, but Kevin is getting remarried to—"

"It's okay. I already saw them together."

The obvious relief on his face was almost comical.

"Then, you know, according to the will, Kevin will get everything. And he is planning to sell the pharmacy and let some developer bulldoze the place."

"Oh, Trevor. I'm so sorry."

"I'm glad you feel that way because I can't let my brother do that. And that's where you come in."

"Me?"

"Yes."

"What can I possibly do to help?"

"You can marry me."

Chapter Four

TREVOR

ALEXIS'S brown eyes got so big that I worried they would come out of her head, and I realized I could have sprung the marriage thing on her better.

"I know it seems kind of out there—"

"Kind of?" she interrupted.

I smiled. "Okay, it's very out there, but I don't know what else to do. I can't let Kevin inherit the business. People in that town count on it for employment and prescriptions. Marriage is my best option."

She put a hand on her hip. "And you thought of me?"

"Yes. I'm not dating anyone currently, so who better to ask than someone who doesn't like my brother?"

She snorted. " 'Doesn't like' is an understatement."

"Even better," I joked.

Alexis didn't laugh. "I know I hate Kevin, but how does this benefit me? It seems as though I'm going to end up being twice divorced with two ex-husbands when this is all over."

"One ex-husband. You and I can apply for an annulment."

She slowly nodded her head. "Okay. Keep talking."

"If you marry me, I will hire an attorney for you. I'm probably going to need a lawyer anyway to fight my brother after my grandma passes." She opened her mouth, and I held up my hand before she could protest, like she had to her friend. "Before you say no, helping you get your money is what I will do if you help me inherit the pharmacy. Tit for tat. I can't ask you to help me like this without giving you something in return."

She opened her mouth again, but I was so worried she was going to turn me down that I kept talking.

"Kevin is going to be suspicious of this arrangement, and we're going to have to convince him we're a love match. If I don't help you get your half of the house from him, he might suspect our marriage is temporary."

"I agree."

My eyes widened. "You do?"

"Yes. If you had let me speak, I would have told you, I'm in."

I winced. "Sorry about that. I just figured you were going to tell me no."

She frowned.

"I heard you and your friend out there," I explained.

"How much did you listen to?"

"Enough. You were speaking out in the open." I hadn't been trying to spy on her or anything. "Can I ask why you said yes to me but no to her?"

"Looking a gift horse in the mouth, are we?"

"How about we just say, my curiosity is piqued?"

She lifted a shoulder. "It's not just about me. Your grandparents were never anything but nice to me, and even though they won't be around to see what happens to the pharmacy, it still breaks my heart. I know how much that place means to them. Also, I can't deny that I want to see the look on Kevin's face when he finds out you're married and all his plans are ruined. But then to find out I'm taking him to court too? He's going to be so mad."

She grinned, and I couldn't fault her for feeling spiteful.

"And then there's you..." she added.

I furrowed my brow. *Me?* "What about me?"

"You were always a better person than your brother, and you never took his side when we got divorced. I know he asked you for a statement or something, but you declined."

I looked away. I hadn't realized that she knew that, and I was embarrassed that my brother had even asked me.

I turned back to her. "I wasn't going to lie."

"Exactly. And that's why you deserve to inherit the business and not Kevin."

"Thank you. But we'll jointly inherit the place since we'll both meet the will's requirements."

"I know, but this way, you'll have a fighting chance of keeping it out of someone else's hands. You'd better get us a really good lawyer. And speaking of a lawyer, we should do a prenup."

I knew she was right, but I shook my head. "No. If Kevin finds out we did a prenup, he might be unconvinced of our relationship. All it would take is for his own attorney to find the paperwork. If we end up going to court to fight over the business, I don't want him to win because he proved our marriage was fake."

She shrugged. "I don't have anything anyway—unless you want my crappy apartment and my old car."

I looked around. "Except your business."

She laughed. "My business partners are rich and could hire a dozen lawyers that would demolish you in court. I'm not worried."

My eyebrows flew up. "Noted."

"But we should do the prenup anyway. That way, Kevin can't say I married you for your business."

She had a good point.

"Okay, you're right."

"Good. When do you want to do this?"

"As soon as possible. I don't know how long my grandma actually has."

Alexis reached behind her, untied her apron, and let

down her wavy, dark hair. "Let's go then," she said, pulling the smock over her head.

"Now?"

"You said as soon as possible. Possible is already here. One of our two employees should be here soon, so I have some free time right now."

"Okay. Let's do this."

I followed Alexis out of the kitchen and to the front.

"Tessa, I need to leave for a bit."

Her friend she had been speaking to earlier lifted her head from the bakery case. "Where are you going?"

"To get a marriage license."

Tessa's jaw dropped. "I thought you said you were never getting married again."

"I should have clarified. I'm never getting married again for love. This time, I'm getting married for revenge."

Tessa blinked at her. "Revenge?"

"I'll explain later." Alexis snapped her fingers as a thought came to her. "But that reminds me. Can you ask Seth for a good attorney who could fit in Trevor and me today?"

Chapter Five

ALEXIS

"YOU KNOW, there's a preapplication you have to fill out online, and you have to schedule an appointment," Tessa said.

"I should have known." I turned on my heel toward our office. "Come on, Trevor."

Tessa and I had chosen an L-shaped desk so that we could both sit and work if we needed to, which also came in handy when applying for a marriage application.

I got behind the computer, and with a quick Google search, I found our county's website and information.

"What's your middle name?" I asked. "Funny. I should probably already know that."

"William."

"You were named after your grandfather? How sweet."

Trevor tilted his head. "Is it when he's the reason we're doing this?"

"How ironic? Is that better?"

"I don't think that's it either."

"You're probably right." I typed in Trevor's full name. *Trevor William Nelson.*

Next was birthdate and sex.

"You know my birthday?" Trevor asked, and I blushed.

"You were my husband's brother. It was my job to know when your birthday was."

"That makes sense."

Good. Because I didn't want him to know I had already remembered it from before I got married. Trevor's birthday was when I'd met him after all. But that had probably slipped his mind.

"I need your address, county, phone number, and email address. For the marriage certificate and for me."

"Yeah, it's probably a good idea to know my future wife's information."

After we put our info into each other's phones, I returned to where I'd left off on the application, completing Trevor's information. I clicked no for the question asking if Trevor had been previously married, and then I moved on to enter my information.

"Alexis Grace Moore," Trevor said, reading over my shoulder. "You changed your name back after you got divorced?"

"Actually, I never changed it in the first place."

"Yes, you did."

I laughed. "Nope."

"Wow."

I looked over my shoulder at him. "What?"

"Nothing. Maybe you knew the marriage wouldn't last."

I leaned toward him. "Or maybe I'm a modern woman who thinks changing my last name is archaic and misogynistic."

He shrugged. "Maybe it was both."

"You're not going to call me out for being a feminist or anything?"

He frowned. "Why? It's just a last name."

"Your brother did."

"I thought we'd already established that I'm a better person than him."

I smiled. "Touché." I turned back to the computer and finished my portion of the application.

The next section made me laugh. It just happened to be about what we wanted our names to be after we were married.

"So, do you want to be Trevor Moore?" I joked.

"Tempting, but Nelson goes with the name of the family business."

"Right. It probably wouldn't look good if you changed your last name before fighting for Nelson Pharmacy."

"You got that right."

I typed in Trevor's name the same as previously, but

when I got to my part, I put down Nelson for my last name.

Trevor leaned forward. "What are you doing?"

"Putting down my future last name."

"But you didn't change it with my brother."

"And won't that really piss him off?"

"I think I might be getting married to somebody evil."

I looked him in the eyes. "Don't cross me, and you'll be just fine."

The corner of his mouth tilted up. "Good to know."

I looked away and licked my lips. *Is Trevor flirting with me? Probably not.*

I regrouped my thoughts and moved on. "Address after marriage?"

We hadn't talked about this yet.

"My house. Unless…"

"I live in a tiny-ass apartment, courtesy of your brother."

"Well, not any longer."

I tapped the keyboard and bit my lip. "Are you sure you're okay with me moving in? That's a big change. I can stay at my place."

Trevor's brow furrowed, and he almost looked angry, but I didn't feel like it was directed toward me.

"Is my brother or anyone else going to believe that we're married if we live separately?"

"No."

"Then, you're moving in."

Filling out the application was the easy part. Trying to find an appointment was a headache. And this was just to get the license.

"A month? We can't wait a month," Trevor said. "My grandma will likely have only a month or two to live."

"Don't panic yet. We have a few more places we can book an appointment." I clicked on another location. "This one is in two weeks."

"Better."

"I'll keep looking."

On the fifth one, I got lucky.

"This one has an appointment tomorrow morning." I checked the address. "It's a bit of a drive to get there, but—"

"Do it."

"Done. But next, we have to schedule our ceremony."

This required a couple of phone calls, but we were able to get in two days later.

I set my phone down and slumped in my chair. "I'm tired, and we haven't even done anything yet."

Trevor stood, giving me a full shot of his amazing package. I could see the outline of his dick pressed up against his gray pants, and I tried not to stare.

The night I had met Trevor and Kevin, they had gone skinny-dipping. I wouldn't say that I had first been attracted to Trevor over his brother because of what he carried in his pants, but it sure hadn't hurt.

"Alexis?"

Crap. I hadn't looked away fast enough. I hoped he hadn't caught me.

"Yeah?"

Trevor held out his hand. "Let's go."

Pushing myself off my chair, I asked, "Where are we going?"

"There's something else we need to do before we get married."

"We don't have a lawyer yet."

"Not that." He took my hand. "Something else."

He led me out of the office, his palm warm and secure. It was nice to be single, but I sometimes forgot the good things about being in a relationship.

"Where are you going?" Tessa asked when we passed her.

I lifted my free hand and shrugged. "I don't know."

———

"Pick out any one you want."

I laughed and looked up at Trevor, thinking he was joking.

His face was serious.

"I'm not going to pick out a ring."

Had this man forgotten that this was a fake marriage? It seemed so since he had dragged me to a jewelry store. I knew Trevor had money from his parents passing away and had a good job, but he didn't need to get me anything.

He shifted toward the sales attendant. "We have a short engagement—very short—and we need wedding rings. Is there anything you can do for us?" He looked at me again. "Are you sure there is nothing you want to request?"

There was something I had wanted with Kevin, but he hadn't gotten it for me.

"Tell me."

"I always wanted black diamonds or a black ring." I quickly turned to the salesclerk. "But if you don't have anything, it's okay. I'll wear whatever."

The woman smiled and held up her finger. "One moment. I'll be right back."

She moved down the long display and opened a drawer underneath. She pulled out a few things and brought them back to us.

"We had these out, but there wasn't much interest in them, so we made room for new inventory." She opened the first box and set it in front of us. Then, she opened the second and set it next to the first.

"They're beautiful," I whispered.

They were both silver in color with black diamonds. I wasn't good with identifying if something was made out of silver, white gold, or platinum. The woman's ring had a black solitaire princess cut diamond with black baguette diamonds on the sides. The man's ring was thick with a line of small black diamonds in the center with black baguette diamonds on each side.

"Are they white gold?" I asked.

"Platinum."

I took a step back. Platinum was much more expensive.

"We'll take them," Trevor said.

The saleswoman looked alarmed. "Don't you want to try them on?"

"Nah, we're good. I'm a size ten. Alexis?"

"Seven."

"When can you have them ready?" Trevor asked her.

"In a day or two."

"Perfect."

Chapter Six

ALEXIS

"I NOW PRONOUNCE you husband and wife. I just need you and your witnesses to sign the paperwork, and we will get that filed for you," the justice of the peace said.

It was Saturday morning, and I watched my new husband—something I'd never thought I'd say again—sign his name on the dotted line.

I signed after him, and I turned the marriage certificate over to Pru. "Thanks for being my witness today."

"I still can't believe you're doing this, but I'm happy to help out." She scribbled her name on the witness line. "I hope this gets what is owed to you."

"It will." Trevor took the marriage certificate from Pru. "I'll make sure of it." He handed it to his friend, who was our other witness. "Here you go."

While both men were looking the other way, Pru wiggled her eyebrows at me and mouthed, *That's hot.*

She wasn't wrong. His determination to do right by me was pretty hot. He also looked good. He wore a pair of black slacks and a gray button-down shirt. I was glad that I had worn something a little fancier than jeans.

I shook my head. *It's not real*, I mouthed back.

She rolled her eyes. *Right*. "Just look at Bree and Zack."

"Who's Bree and Zack?" Trevor asked.

"Our friends," I quickly said before Pru could say more. "They're getting married soon," I added because I couldn't come up with anything good to justify why we had been talking about them.

Pru snort-laughed into her fist but quickly composed herself. Pulling her phone out of her purse, she said, "Let me take a picture of the two newlyweds."

"That's a good idea." Trevor put his arm around me and pulled me to his side. "Smile like I love you," he joked.

I laughed. "How about I smile like I'm about to crush my ex?"

He grinned. "Even better."

"Hold up your hand," Pru said.

I wiggled my ring finger for the camera.

"That's very pretty."

"Alexis picked it out," Trevor told Pru.

Pru gave me a look, but I shook my head.

She took a few pictures of us and studied her work. "These look great. I'll send them to you, Alexis. But I need to get to work. I have to meet a bride and her mother in twenty minutes."

I gave her a hug and sent her on her way while Trevor said good-bye to his friend.

"Can your friend be trusted to keep our secret?" Trevor asked.

"Definitely. She hates Kevin just as much as I do."

He nodded. "Good."

"What about your friend?"

"He'll keep his mouth shut."

"Great." I looked around, not sure what to do. There was no handbook on what to say to your husband who wasn't a real husband after you got married. "So, what do we do now?" I asked.

"Go home." He looked at his watch. "The movers are supposed to show up in an hour or so."

"Right. Home."

Trevor's home was my home now. My, how my life had changed in the last few days.

Just like the day he had come to my café, Trevor took my hand and led me out into the hall. We continued out to the parking lot, and he didn't let go until we got to his car. I liked to think that holding hands was Trevor's thing, but I was sure it was all for show.

We rode to his house in silence, and it was soon apparent that this was going to be an awkward marriage. The last few days, we had been busy, setting the appointment at the courthouse, picking out rings, getting our marriage license, speaking to a lawyer and signing papers, and planning my move to his house. With nothing more to do, we didn't have much to talk about.

Thankfully, I got a text from Pru with the pictures she had taken. I did a double take when I first pulled them up. I thought I had done a good job of acting like it was the happiest day of my life. But Trevor...Trevor was a great actor. He looked like he couldn't wait to get me home and consummate our marriage. No, that was too tame. He looked like he wanted to take me home and fuck me until I forgot my name.

I slammed the phone down on my lap.

Trevor glanced down and up to my face. "Are you okay?"

"Yeah. Just realizing how real this all is."

He adjusted in his seat. "I understand that. With all the planning, it almost seemed surreal."

"And now, it's just real."

I picked up my cell again and looked at what were my wedding photos and sighed.

At the end of my marriage to Kevin, it had been obvious we were headed toward divorce. We hadn't had sex in months, and even before then, it had been weeks apart when we did. The last couple of months, we started sleeping in separate beds. Kevin had claimed his back hurt, so he went to the guest room, and I hadn't stopped him. Even though I wasn't in love anymore, I had been lonely. It'd turned out, being alone made me feel less lonely than being married to Kevin had.

I had forgotten how much I had felt like that until right this moment.

Studying Trevor's face and the heat in his eyes reminded me all over again of how I had been in a loveless marriage. I had known that going in, obviously, so why it felt like a revelation, I didn't know.

But it sure felt like crap.

"Pru sent the photos she took of us," I said, needing to do something to distract me from feeling sorry for myself. "Do you want me to send them to you, so you can send them to your family?" We both knew I was really talking about Kevin.

Trevor scratched his five o'clock shadow. It wasn't really a five o'clock shadow. He kept his facial hair short and trimmed, and that was the best description of it. "What do all the kids do these days with news like that?" he joked. In a serious voice, he said, "Since we didn't tell many people about the wedding, post it on social media."

My mouth fell open. "That's how you're going to tell your brother?"

"Maybe. If he doesn't call me or come by the house in a few days, I'll invite him over for dinner." Trevor laughed. "He's going to flip his shit."

I laughed too, feeling better. This was why I was doing this. Watching my ex be miserable was going to be worth it.

Pulling up every social media site I had an account on, I posted the pictures, tagging Trevor where I could. I even put them on Twitter, which I hadn't posted on in almost a year. As I went to my home screen, a thought occurred to me.

"I immediately regret what I did."

Trevor's eyes got huge, and he looked alarmed.

I didn't think my statement was that big of a deal, so I continued on. "I'm going to get an abundance of notifications soon. I'd best prepare for the questions of how and when."

He relaxed. "Yes, we are going to have to field a lot from friends and family."

My phone rang in my hands.

"Uh-oh. Kevin isn't the only one who's going to lose his shit."

"Who is it?"

"My mother. I might have forgotten to tell my parents about the wedding." I bit my lip. "What do I tell them?"

"Does your family like Kevin?"

I snorted.

"Then, tell them the truth."

"Right." I hit the Answer button and lifted the phone to my ear. "Hi, Mom."

"Don't you *Mom* me, young lady. You got married? To

your ex-husband's brother? And didn't even tell me? I had to find out through Facebook."

Yikes. She was mad.

I glanced at Trevor and realized the truth might be worse than fiction. I'd never told her that Kevin hadn't given me all the money he owed me in the divorce, and I didn't want to upset her by telling her that news too.

"I'm sorry, Mom. I know it seems crazy, but Trevor and I met up again, and we decided we'd already wasted enough years being apart. Why wait, ya know?" I chuckled nervously.

"Honey, I know you originally liked Trevor before Kevin when you first met them back in the day, but people change. Are you sure this is wise? He might not be the same person anymore."

My eyes flew to Trevor. Had he heard what my mom said about him? I didn't want him to know I'd had a crush on him first when he never liked me back. The embarrassment of then marrying his brother and it all going to hell was even worse.

Thankfully, Trevor was staring straight out the window.

"Yes, I know people change. Some for the better."

"Honey—"

"Look, let's talk about this later, okay? We'll have dinner this week."

"If you think I'm going to be less upset if you wait a few days, think again."

"I would never."

"Dinner on Wednesday. Six sharp."

"Yes, ma'am."

"And bring your new husband."

Click.

My phone was flashing when I looked at it, indicating what I'd already known. She'd hung up.

"Decided to lie?"

"Yes. It's a long story."

"You're helping me out. I'm not going to judge."

"Good. Because we have to do dinner on Wednesday. I hope you're ready to re-meet your new in-laws."

Chapter Seven

TREVOR

LOOKING OUT THE WINDOW, I frowned at the size of the moving truck that backed into my driveway. It didn't look big enough to hold a whole apartment's worth of things.

"Your stuff is here," I called out to Alexis.

She had packed some clothes in her car and was putting them away in the spare bedroom. We had already decided it would be believable for her to have her own closet in the other room. And it was logical for Alexis to bring her old bed and put it in the room for guests. We had tried to justified everything in case my brother found a way to snoop around. And if he did, hopefully, it wasn't at night to catch her sleeping in her own bed.

Alexis bounced down the stairs. "Great."

We went outside together to greet the movers and to direct them on where to put her things.

I watched them carry in a bed, a dresser, and less than ten boxes.

"Where's the rest of your stuff?" I asked, walking into Alexis's new room.

She looked up from a box she'd opened. "What do you mean?"

"You had to have more than a bed at your apartment."

She cringed. "Oh, I did, but you don't want any of that stuff in this nice house. My furniture is awful. Old and a lot of hand-me-downs. The only thing I spent money on was my mattress, and even that wasn't a lot."

I gritted my teeth and tried not to curse. When she had lived with my brother, she'd had a nice house with beautiful furniture. Not only did my brother make good money, but both of us also had money from when our parents had passed and from our father's shares of pharmacy. It had been put into a trust that gave us funds every month. Neither of us was hurting for money. Kevin didn't need to swindle his ex-wife out of her settlement money.

"What an ass." I couldn't bite my tongue.

Alexis lifted her head. "What?"

"Nothing." I didn't want her to feel worse about her decision to marry Kevin. "So, what did you do with the things you didn't move?"

Her brow furrowed. "I left them at the apartment. I didn't think it made sense to move everything when I'm going to go back soon."

I sighed, feeling bad for her. "If my brother does any digging, he can't see that you still have your apartment half-furnished."

She bit her lip. "You're right. I'm sorry."

I got down on my haunches and lifted her chin. "You don't have to apologize to me. This isn't your fault."

She nodded, but I felt like she didn't agree.

"Also, you have to remember, when this is all over, you will have your money and won't have to move back there."

She smiled, but it didn't quite reach her eyes. "You're right. I keep forgetting that."

"Do you want me to call the moving company back?"

Grimacing, she said, "No. Like I said, my stuff wouldn't fit in with your things. I'll donate it."

"Hey, good idea." I stood. "How many months left on your lease?"

"Uh...two, I think."

"I'll take care of that for you."

She jumped up. "You don't have to do that. I can pay the—"

Ding-dong, ding-dong, ding-dong, ding-dong.

Alexis and I locked eyes.

"I think your brother's here," she whispered.

Boom, boom, boom.

He'd gone from ringing the bell to pounding on the door.

"That was sooner than I'd expected." I exhaled a whoosh of air. "Here goes nothing."

The doorbell was ringing again as I walked down the stairs.

"I'm coming. You can stop now. I know you're there," I yelled.

Swinging open the front door, I was ready to confront my brother, but I wasn't ready for who was actually on the other side.

"*You got married?*" My ex-girlfriend, Lorraine, pushed past me and walked in.

"Come in," I said sarcastically.

"Trevor, how could you?" she whined.

"Lorraine, we haven't dated for two years." I was completely baffled as to why she was so upset.

"But we always get back together, Trevor."

I could see where she had a point, but she was delusional if she thought I was ever going to marry her. "Yes, we dated on and off for many years. But we've never gone this long without getting back together. I thought it was clear that we were over."

A movement out of the corner of my eye caught my attention.

I motioned for Alexis to come over.

My new wife came to my side and slipped her arms around me. I had always been affectionate with the women

I dated, and Lorraine would know that. I kissed Alexis on the top of her head because this woman understood the assignment.

"Lorraine, you remember Alexis?"

Lorraine scoffed. "Don't you think this situation is weird?"

My ex and I had dated while Alexis was still married to Kevin. We had even gone on a few couples dates together, so it was a little weird.

Alexis shrugged. "The heart doesn't care what's weird and what's not. It just knows it's in love."

I squeezed her side. "Good answer, babe." I'd added the nickname at the last minute. It felt right.

"Besides, aren't you engaged to someone, Lorraine? You have it posted all over social media," Alexis said, turning toward her with a hand on her hip.

"Yes, but..."

"But you still hoped that Trevor and you would get back together someday?"

Lorraine looked away.

"I don't blame you," Alexis said. "This man is a keeper. But you can't have two men." She paused. "I mean, you can. If they are both up for a polyamorous relationship. But I'm guessing your fiancé isn't interested." She leaned forward and lowered her voice. "And we both know Trevor doesn't like to share." She straightened. "So, I guess the only thing I have to say is, you snooze, you lose. Finders keepers, losers weepers."

"I am not some prize, Alexis," I joked.

She laid her head on my chest. "You're right, honey; you're not." She lifted her head again. "Sorry, Lorraine, but he's mine."

I laughed. "Did you need anything else?" I asked my ex. "Because we need to finish unpacking some of Alexis's stuff, and it is our wedding night."

"No." Lorraine headed to the door. "I think I just wanted to see if it was true."

"It is," Alexis said. "Thanks for coming though."

My ex left without another word, and Alexis stepped away from me.

"I guess that was good practice for when Kevin comes around."

"Yeah."

"Were you surprised to see her?"

"Very. We've been over for a long time."

"That's good. She was never good enough for you."

My eyebrows rose. I'd never realized Alexis felt that way.

"I suppose I should get back to unpacking."

"Alexis?" I said before she left.

"What?"

"How did you know I don't like to share?"

She smiled. "I know you, I guess."

Part of me didn't think it was an unreasonable thing to know about me. Another part of me couldn't believe she knew that.

"Yeah, I guess..." I shook off my thoughts. "You'd better go finish unpacking. I'm sure my brother will show up soon."

Chapter Eight

ALEXIS

TREVOR and I both retired for the night without a word from Kevin. It was a shock since he wasn't big on social media, but it felt anticlimactic to go to bed without him confronting us.

But one thing I hadn't considered until I pulled back my comforter was that maybe he didn't care. He had thrown our marriage away before we were even separated, so maybe my marriage to his brother didn't bother him even though he would now have to share his inheritance.

I knew I was doing the right thing in helping Trevor, but I was disappointed.

Such was life, I supposed, and I shouldn't be surprised that I had lost out again when it came to my ex-husband.

Amazingly, I had fallen asleep hard and fast, but I woke up a couple hours later in full alert mode.

I wasn't sure what had woken me until I heard a banging at the front door. The hall light flipped on, and I saw Trevor walking past in only a pair of pajama pants.

My heart began to beat fast. It had to be Kevin at the door. I didn't know anyone else who would be outside the house at midnight.

I slipped out of bed and tiptoed to the edge of the hallway to listen.

"I'm coming," Trevor bit out as the sound of the front door opened. "What?"

"Don't *what* me," a familiar voice said. "I just got a phone call, telling me my wife married my brother."

I held my breath as I waited for Trevor's response.

"She's not your wife anymore, man. She's mine. You didn't want her, remember?"

"She left me."

"No, she didn't."

"She left my bed. That's the same thing," Kevin said.

"Only after you treated her like shit. Why do you care anyway? You're getting married to someone else soon."

"That's not the point."

"Then, what is?" Trevor sounded like he was tired of the situation. "You don't own Alexis. She can marry whoever she wants."

"How did this even happen? How did you two even

get..." Kevin trailed off and gasped. "This is about Nana." He laughed. "I should have known. You don't even like Alexis. You just married her to get the pharmacy."

I flinched at hearing Kevin say Trevor didn't like me, and I tried to push it away because the bigger factor was that Kevin had figured out Trevor's plan. We had expected it, but it was going to take some convincing to prove we were a real couple.

"I admit, we might have gotten married sooner than normal—Alexis doesn't want you ruining our legacy either —but we were already a couple and would have gotten married eventually anyway."

"Ooh...smart," I whispered to myself.

Admitting part of the truth made it more believable. We hadn't discussed it, but I thought Trevor had made the right decision.

"I don't believe you," Kevin said.

"Don't believe what?"

"That you two are in a relationship."

"You don't have to believe it, but it's true."

"When our grandmother passes, I'm going to prove that your marriage is a sham."

The front door closed, and there was a shuffling sound.

"You're not going up there, Kevin."

Shit. If he came up here, he was going to see that I was in my own bed.

"And why not? Because you don't want me to see that you and Alexis aren't sleeping together?"

I spun around and quickly made my bed. I grabbed my phone and the glass of water I had sitting on the nightstand and carefully slid out into the hall. I bolted toward Trevor's room while trying to be light on my feet. It wasn't easy, and my heart was racing when I got there, but I made it.

"I'm not letting you disturb my wife. She's sleeping."

Kevin snorted. "You're a liar."

I went to the unslept-on side of the king-sized bed and set my things down as if I had put them there before going to sleep. I stripped off my pajamas and looked around. *Would I have taken my PJs off before bed, or would my new husband have taken them off for me?*

"You can't stop me." Kevin's voice was louder and closer than before.

I didn't have time to worry about where my clothes landed. I just threw them on the floor and slipped under the covers just as footsteps pounded on the stairs.

Laying my head on the pillow, I did my best to pretend like I'd been sleeping.

"*Aha...*" Kevin said.

I half-opened one eye and put my hand up, as if the hall light were too bright for me. "What's going on?" I asked in the best scratchy-from-sleep voice I could come up with.

"My brother doesn't believe we're a real couple," Trevor said.

I sat up to lean against the headboard, letting the sheet slip off of my chest just enough to show a breast. I figured Kevin had already seen them, and maybe knowing I was naked would help convince him that our marriage was genuine.

Rubbing my eyes, I said, "Sorry to break it to you, Kevin, but Trev and I are the real deal."

"Trev? You two are on a nickname basis now?"

"Lexie and I are a couple, so yeah."

Kevin laughed. "You messed up. Alexis hates being called Lexie."

Fuck. I always went by Alexis, but Trevor probably hadn't known that about me.

I needed to salvage this.

I yawned like Kevin hadn't caught us. "Listen, Trevor makes me come—unlike you. He can call me whatever he wants." I pushed my body back down and got comfortable, as if I were bored with the conversation. "Now, go away, Kevin, so my husband can come back and make love to me again."

Kevin pointed his finger at me. "This isn't over. I'm going to prove this is a fake marriage."

I rolled my eyes and looked at Trevor. "Hurry back," was the only thing I said.

Trevor grabbed the back of Kevin's neck. "It's time for you to leave. It's late."

He managed to get his brother to turn and go back downstairs, and I sighed with relief. That could have gone horribly bad, but I thought Trevor and I had done pretty well.

The two brothers talked more. I couldn't make out what they were saying, but with Kevin still in the house, I didn't want to get up and go back to my room, so I closed my eyes in case he came back upstairs.

Now that I was alone, I noticed how comfortable Trevor's bed was. When I got my divorce money from Kevin, I was going to buy a bed just like this. I smiled as I pictured my ex reluctantly handing me a check.

That was the image I fell asleep to.

Chapter Nine

TREVOR

I WATCHED my new wife walk down the stairs, fully clothed, while I hid my erection behind the kitchen island.

I knew I wasn't supposed to be attracted to Alexis, but my body did not care. I couldn't get the image of her beautiful breast and dark rosy nipple out of my head. It didn't help that I'd had to sleep next to her naked body all night. My saving grace had been my big king-sized bed and the ability to put some space between the two of us.

But I also couldn't get her words out of my head. *"Listen, Trevor makes me come—unlike you. He can call me whatever he wants."*

I shouldn't have been surprised my brother was a selfish lover, but I was.

One thing for sure was, I needed to stop thinking about Alexis in a sexual way, or I was going to be miserable throughout this whole marriage.

"Sorry about calling you Lexie last night," I told her as she took a seat at the counter.

"It's fine. I'm just hoping my reason for being okay with it was believable."

I took a sip of my coffee. "He wouldn't have believed us, regardless of what we said. Coffee?"

"Yes, please."

Opening the cupboard, I got a mug out for her and poured her coffee. "I admit, I panicked when he bolted past me and actually went up the stairs. I didn't know how I was going to explain you being in a different bed. Thanks for being quick on your feet. No pun intended."

She smiled as I pushed her cup over to her and leaned on the counter with my elbows. "I'm just glad I woke up when he got here. But I'm sorry I didn't go back to my room after he left. I fell asleep. Your bed is so comfortable."

I didn't know what possessed me to say what I said next, but I opened my mouth and told her, "It's not a problem. You can sleep there every night if you want. It might be smart. I wouldn't put it past Kevin to use his key to sneak in while we're sleeping."

"I agree since I'm pretty sure we didn't convince him."

"Yeah, he's an asshole, but he's pretty smart. He was definitely still skeptical when he left."

Lifting her coffee to her lips, she met my eyes. "Does this mean we should also sleep naked?" she joked.

I raised an eyebrow. My dick liked that idea.

She looked away and cleared her throat. "I'm sorry. That was inappropriate."

I'd embarrassed her. "No, no, it's fine. We are husband and wife after all."

"Only in the loosest sense of the words."

I frowned, her statement sitting wrong with me for some reason. "I'll get the locks changed right away. My brother shouldn't be able to get in, no matter what."

"I appreciate that." She took a drink. "What did Kevin say to you after you left the bedroom?"

I sighed. "Just that he wasn't going to hand over the inheritance to me."

"What did you say?"

"That I didn't expect any less from him. And then he said he was going to prove that we only got married because of the will."

"Do you think he'll be able to do that?"

"I'm going to do my best so he can't."

"Do you really believe you'd lose the business if he was able to prove it?"

"That all depends on how good our lawyers are and what the judge thinks. Technically, the will never said the marriage had to be real, but one could argue that a fake marriage doesn't count. Bottom line: I don't want to risk it."

"I understand. I will do whatever you need for this to be a real marriage."

"Thank you. And I'll do what it takes to get you your money."

Alexis looked away. "Do you think maybe we should find out some more things about each other? Like, intimately?"

"You mean, so we don't have another nickname mishap?"

"Yes."

"You realize I'm going to have to call you Lexie now. At least sometimes."

She chuckled. "I know. I don't really hate it. I just prefer my full name instead."

"Noted. I'll only call you Lexie during private moments."

Her eyes widened, and I laughed.

"I mean, in front of my brother, for things like, *Lexie, it's time for bed.*"

She shivered.

I frowned. "Is that okay?"

"Yes. That's just fine."

I wasn't convinced. "You let me know if it's not."

"I will. We should probably also discuss PDA. Neither of us wants to do something the other doesn't like and have Kevin call us out on it."

"You're right." I rubbed my chin. "I like holding hands."

"I noticed."

"Do you not?"

"Oh, no. I do too."

Whew. I would have been disappointed if I'd had to give that up.

Alexis slid off her stool. "Can you come over here?"

"Sure."

I walked to her side of the counter, and she slid her arm in mine.

"Is this okay?"

"Yes." I put my arm around her. "How about this?"

"Fine by me."

"Okay if we keep going?" I asked to make sure she really was okay even if it had been her idea.

"Yep."

Taking a step away, I put my hand on the small of her back. "Is this okay? I know some women don't like it."

She held up a finger. "A lot of women don't like it when random men do it. But if you're dating me or if you're my husband, it's perfectly acceptable."

"Noted." I moved close, slid my arm around her front, and drew her back to me. "Is this okay?"

Her answer was breathy and low.

"Can you repeat that?"

"Yes, it's fine." She relaxed in my hold.

I hadn't realized she'd been stiff at first, so I squeezed

her middle to let her know she was safe with me. I liked how she felt in my arms.

She moved impossibly closer, and my shaft immediately got the wrong idea.

I jerked back and quickly moved around to her front to face her. "Did we get everything?" I tried to make my voice as even as possible because I was feeling anything but calm.

She stepped toward me and wrapped her arms around me. She was warm and soft and felt too good. "Seems like hugging makes sense."

"Right," I said, trying to keep my pelvis from hitting hers.

She slid her arms up to my neck and smiled. "This is going to take some getting used to."

She has no idea.

"For sure. Anything else?" I sure hoped she was done. I didn't want to be rude, but my dick was starting to ache.

She laid her head on my chest. "Just the usual when couples are close like this. Are you doing okay?"

"Yep." My voice sounded like an adolescent boy's.

She slid her head up and ran her nose against my neck.

I was going to die.

Her breath fanned over my skin, and I was done.

Putting my hands on her upper arms, I gently pushed her back. "Okay, I think we're good here. I need to go and take a shower." A cold one.

"Oookay." She drew out the word, sounding confused, and I felt bad, but I needed to get out of there.

"We'll talk later." I took off and bolted up the stairs and straight into my bathroom.

Even with the shower at near freezing temps, I still had to take my cock in my hand and finish myself off.

Chapter Ten

ALEXIS

I WIPED the steam off the mirror in the bathroom and sighed.

Turning left and right, I studied my reflection. I knew I wasn't the prettiest woman in the world, but I didn't think I was repulsive enough to run away from either.

I had thought Trevor and I were having fun that morning, testing out how much affection we could show one another, until he suddenly bolted.

And since I knew he wasn't a blushing virgin, it had to be because I'd made him uncomfortable. Was he worried I would get attached to him?

It had been years and years ago that I told Kevin I was interested in Trevor, and Kevin went to find out if Trevor felt the same. When he came back, he told me that Trevor didn't like me like that. It had broken my teenage heart, and Kevin had promised he didn't tell Trevor that I was the one asking, but knowing Kevin like I did now, there was a strong chance he had actually told Trevor I liked him. It had happened over a decade ago, and I had ended up dating and marrying Kevin, but there was a chance Trevor remembered what Kevin had said and was worried I'd develop feelings for him again.

I would hope he knew I was smarter than that nineteen-year-old girl, but maybe I needed to make it clear that I understood the marriage was fake and was going to stay that way.

One thing for sure was, this man had my head all twisted. This was why I had decided I wasn't dating or planning to get married again, yet here I was.

I pulled on my clothes and combed through my hair. I needed a good reminder that I shouldn't worry what this guy thought of me. I didn't need to do all the right things to keep him. Which meant that I should march downstairs and tell him he didn't need to worry.

I finished getting ready and headed downstairs to find Trevor. He was standing in front of the kitchen screen door, staring outside.

"Hey," I said as I entered the room.

He glanced over his shoulder, a heavy look on his face.

"What's wrong?"

"When I called my grandmother to invite her over for dinner this weekend to tell her about us, she insisted that we visit her instead. Apparently, Kevin has some big news, but we both know what that news is going to be."

We do?

"That he's going to tell your grandma before we can just to piss you off?" I asked as I came to stand beside him.

"Huh. I didn't even think of that. Especially considering how Nana feels about your divorce."

What? How does Nana feel? I wanted to ask but didn't want to interrupt.

"But I think he's going to tell us he's getting married to your former exchange student."

"You mean, your grandma doesn't know yet? Candace looks like she's ready to pop." Leave it to my ex to wait until the last minute.

"Yeah, Kevin said it took some time to get her paperwork to get her back into the country."

I snorted. "Seems like a shitty reason to not tell Grandma."

"I agree. He could have told her last week."

"Do you think he's doing this because he knows you're going to tell her about us?"

"Oh, I'm sure of it." He sighed. "It will also give him a reason to observe us and try to catch us."

"Yeah, about that."

He spun toward me. "You're not changing your mind, are you?"

"No. But I want you to know that you don't have to be scared of me."

His brow furrowed, and he chuckled as he looked down at himself and then me, clearly noting our size differences.

"Not like that. I mean, physically."

He tilted his head to the side.

Ugh. I was messing this up.

"Again, not like that." I stopped and took a deep breath. For not wanting to remind him of my teenage self, I wasn't doing a very good job. "I mean, affectionately."

He smiled. "Are you planning to take advantage of me?" he joked.

"No. And I want you to know, I'm not going to think any touching we do in the name of convincing people is actually real. I won't get any ideas about you liking me as more than a friend, so please don't be afraid of pretending we're a couple in front of others."

His smile turned into a frown. "I wasn't worried."

That was good to hear, but it still didn't explain him running away from me.

"Where is this coming from?"

Yeah, right. I wasn't going to point out he'd left me standing in the middle of the room like a fool.

"Nowhere. It was a thought that came to me while showering. Sometimes, I overthink in there."

He furrowed his brow. "You're sure that's all?"

My phone beeped in my pocket before I could answer. It was my mother.

> Mom: I'm making your favorite for dinner on Wednesday. Bring your appetites.

"It's my mom. She said to bring your appetite on Wednesday."

"You can tell her I always do."

I sent my reply and rubbed my forehead. This was one more thing to be stressed about. This arrangement was beginning to feel like more work than it should be.

But there was one good thing about dinner with my parents.

"Wednesday will be a good way for us to practice before dinner with your grandma and Kevin. If my parents suspect something, it won't matter because they'll keep it a secret."

"Yeah. Practice."

I turned to leave, but Trevor stopped me with a hand on my wrist.

"I still think we should try our best," he said, meeting my eyes.

I swallowed hard. "I do too."

He rubbed his thumb over the inside of my arm. "And I promise to not worry about you falling for me."

His touch felt good, and even if he wasn't worried, I suddenly wasn't so sure I shouldn't be.

Chapter Eleven

TREVOR

"NERVOUS?" I asked.

Alexis had been shifting in the passenger seat since we'd gotten in the car to go to her parents' for dinner.

"I'm not exactly excited about lying to my parents."

On Sunday, she had seemed fine with keeping up our ruse in front of them. I wasn't sure what had changed since then.

"We could tell them the truth." I would be disappointed that we wouldn't get to practice before dinner with Nana and Kevin on Saturday, but I didn't want her to be uncomfortable all night.

I flipped on my left turn signal to switch lanes. As I did that, a black sedan behind me did the same. It was unusual since we were on the interstate, but a voice in my head told me to keep an eye out.

Alexis sighed. "I don't think so. I can already see my

mother's disappointment. She would not approve of us getting married for this reason. She's already excited that I have a chance at love again. I don't want to ruin this for her. Let her have this—for now."

I could understand that, and I didn't blame her. "Tonight will be good practice for dinner with my brother and grandmother," I reminded her. "And we have an appointment on Monday with the lawyer about your case. It will all be worth it."

Her eyes shifted to me and then away. "Right." Her voice was flat, and she seemed unhappy.

Her demeanor and the way she'd been so far this week had me second-guessing the PDA limits we had set with each other.

Last weekend, she'd told me that she was okay with them, but since then, she'd kept her distance from me. It was a polite distance but still a distance. I'd told myself it was because we hadn't gone out in public, but I was beginning to think I was just making excuses. Even if we weren't all over each other at home, she didn't have to stay away from me.

"We could always cancel dinner," I offered.

Her head flipped around incredibly fast. "We can't do that. We're supposed to be there in twenty minutes."

I held up one hand. "It was just an offer. I don't want you to do anything you don't want to do."

"I already told you I'm willing to lie."

"I was more talking about me." I slowed down to turn right, and the black sedan did also. I frowned.

"You? You're uncomfortable with lying to my parents?"

I looked away from my rearview mirror. "I suppose I am, but I was referring to you being uncomfortable around me."

"I'm not uncomfortable being—where are you going? You're not supposed to turn there."

"I think someone's following us."

Alexis gasped and started to turn around.

Quickly, I clamped my hand down on her leg. "Don't turn around. He'll know we know."

She fell back against her seat. "Oh my God. Who would be following us?" She arched her back again just as fast. "Are you a criminal?"

"Really, Alexis? You've known me for a long time."

She threw her hands up. "But it doesn't mean I *know* you. All I know is that I'm not a criminal, so whoever is behind us isn't following me."

I shook my head. "You watch too many movies. I'm not a criminal."

"Then, how do you explain the car? And where are we going to go now? We can't lead them to my parents."

"It's only one person. A guy. And I have a pretty good idea why he's following us."

She gasped again. "So, you lied to me."

"For fuck's sake, I didn't lie. I'd be willing to bet money that my brother hired someone to dig up information on us. Like a private investigator. And that's why we're being followed."

Her mouth opened and closed. "Oh. That's actually a really good theory."

"Ya think?"

"No need to be rude."

"You just called me a liar. And a criminal."

"Sorry about that. I panicked."

"I noticed."

"Ooh, I know how I can get a look." Alexis flipped down her visor and pulled out some lipstick. She pretended to put on her lipstick while her eyes shifted back and forth. "I can't tell much."

"I figured. Does your dad have binoculars?"

She pushed her visor up. "We're still going there?"

"Yes. If I'm right, which I'm ninety-nine percent sure I am, he's not dangerous. But I would like to get a look at him once we get to your parents', see if he parks and watches us. Binoculars would really help."

"I think my dad has a pair."

"Can you find them without asking him? A private investigator might be hard to explain."

"I'm sure I can manage."

"So, if he is doing this for my brother, the best thing we can do is to let him think we haven't noticed him. Which means we're going to have to act like we're in love with each other, even when we're not in front of others."

"That makes sense." She shifted in her seat.

"It's a good thing your parents don't know the truth."

"I agree."

When we turned onto her parents' street, the dark sedan kept going. I felt the tension leave my body and realized I'd been more on edge than I thought.

"The car's gone."

This time, I didn't stop Alexis when she looked behind us. "Do you think it was a coincidence and the person was going the same way?"

I wanted to say yes to put her at ease, but I wasn't sure. "Maybe. Or maybe he knew turning onto a residential street would make him more obvious. Either way, we don't have to worry about him."

I pulled into the driveway of her parents' house and checked the rearview mirror one more time before getting out. I took Alexis's hand, and we walked to the front door.

"We're here," Alexis called out when we entered, and the couple came out from the back of the house.

I had met Alexis's parents a few times when she was married to my brother. They had always seemed nice, but I sensed their wariness as soon as they walked into the room.

I slid my arm around my wife as she said, "Mom, Dad, this is my husband, Trevor. Trevor, these are my parents, Pat and Angie."

"Nice to meet you again," I said, holding out my free hand.

Her parents accepted my gesture and shook my hand, but both of their smiles were only given out of politeness.

"Thanks for having me over for dinner," I said. "It smells delicious in here."

Pat crossed his arms over his chest. "Ang is making her famous pot roast." He narrowed his eyes. "Your brother never liked her pot roast."

I squeezed Alexis closer. "Well, my brother is famous for not knowing a good thing when he has it."

Her dad didn't move while I held my breath.

A few seconds later, he dropped his arms, but his face was still sullen. "Hopefully, you do."

"I assure you, I do."

"We'll see about that." Pat turned and walked away.

Chapter Twelve

ALEXIS

AS MY DAD WALKED AWAY, my mom met my eyes. "Come into the kitchen whenever you're ready. I'll get you two something to drink."

"Thanks, Mom. I'm going to give Trevor a tour first."

My mother followed my dad, and Trevor looked down at me.

"Your father isn't a fan of Kevin, I take it?"

"He hates him." I shrugged. "Not that I can blame him."

He smiled tenderly. "I don't."

I realized that his arm was still around me, so I stepped away. "I think my dad will warm up. Just give him a few..." I trailed off as movement outside the front window caught my eye. I gasped. "Trevor, I think he's back."

Trevor spun around just as a black car parked across

the street. "He's not even trying to hide." He looked back over at me. "I think it's time to find those binoculars."

"They're probably in the basement."

We headed downstairs to the spot where my dad kept his hunting gear and rummaged around.

"Your dad's a hunter?"

"Yeah. He goes out a couple times a year during deer season." I opened up a cabinet and found what I was looking for. "Aha. I found them."

"Great."

When we got back to the main floor, my dad was standing at the top of the stairs. His brow furrowed when he saw what I was holding. "What are you doing with my binoculars?"

"Uh..." I couldn't tell my father someone had been following us. He'd freak out, so I came up with the first thing that popped into my head. "I've started bird-watching, and I wanted to show Trevor a bird outside."

"You started bird-watching?" My father's face was full of skepticism, for which I didn't blame him.

"Uh-huh." I couldn't keep lying, so I stepped around him. "Come on, Trevor. Let's go upstairs and look." I felt my dad's eyes on me until we were out of his sight.

"That was painful and difficult to watch."

"Shut up."

Trevor laughed from behind me.

I led him into the front bedroom. "I got you the binoculars, didn't I?" I pointed out, pushing them against his chest.

"Oof." He took a step back. "Yes, you did."

"So, how do you want to do this?" The window in the bedroom had curtains and blinds that were open. "We probably shouldn't pull the blinds up."

"No. The slots between should be enough."

As Trevor approached the window, I stepped off to the side and against the wall.

"It looks like it's one guy. Blond hair. Thirties, I'm guessing."

"What's he doing?"

"He's on his phone."

"That's not helpful." Everyone was always on their phone.

A few seconds passed.

"He hung up. He's writing something on a notepad. I can't read it."

That seemed a little suspicious. Who drove around with a notepad?

"Holy shit." Trevor pulled the binoculars away for a second and gave me an alarmed look.

"What?"

"I think we can officially say that he's been paid to spy on us. He has a big camera with a long-ass lens."

"No way. Let me look."

Trevor handed me the binoculars, and I stepped in

front of him. I put them up to my eyes, and sure enough, I saw a blond guy with a huge camera.

"It looks like it's straight out of a TV show."

"Except this is real life."

"Yeah. It's weird. I've never been stalked before. Do you think he's a private detective?"

"Has to be. Who else would do something like this?"

I heard Trevor move behind me as I continued to spy on our spy.

"I found him."

I put the binoculars down and looked over my shoulder. "You did?"

"Yep. Kelly Investigations. Jonah Kelly." He flipped his phone around, and I saw a website with a photo that resembled the man sitting outside. "My brother literally went with the first website that popped up on Google."

I turned back to the window. "So, what do we do? Should we confront him?" I laughed. "That would really piss Kevin off."

Trevor chuckled behind me. "It would. But I think we should pretend that we don't know he's out there. We can give him some great intel to send to my brother. Maybe he'll leave us alone then."

"I like that plan."

Kelly, the stalker, moved his camera to the right and left as I watched, pausing every few seconds. If he was looking for juicy info, he wasn't going to find it in my parents' living room.

As soon as the thought left my head, the camera whipped up, and my fight-or-flight kicked in.

"Shit." I flung myself backward to get away from his line of sight, but in my panic, I'd forgotten Trevor was behind me.

I tripped on his foot, causing me to fall into him and knocking us both to the ground. I landed half on top of him, half on the floor, and the binoculars hit me right on the mouth.

"*Owww*," I hissed.

Trevor slid out from under me and leaned over. "Are you okay?"

"The binoculars hit my lip."

My lower body tightened as he stared at my mouth.

"Which lip?"

"My bottom one," I said in a low voice.

He brushed his thumb over it. "Does that hurt?"

"Not really." It felt good. Way too good.

I wanted him to kiss it and make it better.

Bad idea. Especially when it looked like he was thinking the same thing.

"Can you help me sit up?" I asked before my mind could play more tricks on me.

Trevor rolled off and offered me a hand. "What happened?"

Finger-combing the back of my hair, I told him, "He lifted his camera up to the window. I didn't want him to catch me watching him. Sorry I ran into you."

"It's fine. I just want to make sure you're okay."

"All good." I smiled to show him I was serious.

"What are you two doing on the floor?"

We both spun around to see my mom standing in the doorway to the bedroom.

"Your dad said you were bird-watching?" It came out as a question, like she couldn't believe that I would be doing that.

"Uh..." Once again, I didn't know what to say, so out popped the first thing that came to mind. "A bird flew into the window and scared me. I fell down."

Trevor snickered and turned his head away as his shoulders started to shake.

"You need to be more careful, honey," my mom said, ignorant to Trevor's laughing.

"Will do." I lamely gave her a thumbs-up.

"Dinner's ready anyway. Why don't you come downstairs?"

"Be there in a second."

She left to go back downstairs, and Trevor stopped trying to hold back his laugh.

"It's not funny."

He grinned. "It is. Both your parents think you're either lying or something's wrong with you."

I stood. "There is something wrong with me. I married the wrong man, and now, he's spying on me."

Trevor got up too. "It's not all bad. You got me out of the process."

I had to imagine I looked stunned at that statement because we both knew I hadn't actually "gotten" Trevor. He wasn't really mine.

But he must have missed the expression on my face because he said, "I am the handsomer brother after all."

He's joking. That made more sense.

And my hopes—which I hadn't even known I had—sank because for a second there, I'd thought that he really wanted to belong to me.

Chapter Thirteen

ALEXIS

DINNER WENT ABOUT AS WELL as I'd expected it to go. My dad was polite, but I could tell he was just waiting for Trevor to do something, so he could disapprove of our quick marriage. I appreciated that I had a parent who loved me that much, but it actually made the situation more stressful, and I was glad that it was almost over.

"Would you like to stay for dessert?" my mom asked.

Trevor put his hand on my knee and squeezed. My dad's body tensed up. It was apparent the two men wanted dinner to be over.

"They're Alexis's cupcakes," she added. "I bought a couple dozen for work, and I have a few left over."

My poor mother was the only one who wanted us to stay.

"Thanks, Mom, but we're going to call it a night. I need

to get to the bakery early tomorrow for a big order coming in."

My mother's face fell.

"But how about the two of us do something together?" I offered. "We haven't had a mother-daughter date in a while."

She beamed. "I'd like that."

Trevor picked up his napkin from his lap and set it on his empty plate. "Dinner was excellent, Mrs. Moore. Alexis and I will have to have you and Mr. Moore over to our place soon."

"You can call me Angie," she said with a smile and looked over at my dad.

He stood and took his plate to the kitchen.

"I guess you'll be calling him Mr. Moore," I joked to Trevor.

"He'll come around. He just doesn't want his little girl to get hurt again," my mom said, trying to put a positive spin on the evening.

"I know, Mom, and I'm sure Trevor understands."

"I do. If I had a daughter, I'd feel the same, I'm sure." Trevor picked up his plate and got up from the table, but my mom stopped him with a hand.

"No, no, no. You are the guest tonight. You are not helping with dishes."

"My Nana would say otherwise."

"I won't tell her if you don't." My mom winked at him.

"Come on, Trevor. She's never going to let you do it. When she comes to our house, you can return the favor." I dragged him toward the front door with my mom following. "Bye, Dad," I yelled.

I thought he'd ignore me, but he came out of the kitchen and gave me a hug. "I love you."

"I love you too."

"And I know you weren't bird-watching. I'll let it go for now, but I'll want to know what's going on eventually."

"I know."

He let me go. I hugged my mom, and my dad shook my new husband's hand, and then we left.

Jonah Kelly was still outside in his vehicle, so I immediately took Trevor's hand.

"Thanks for coming tonight. I hope you weren't too miserable," I said as we walked to the car.

"I didn't think they'd welcome me with open arms, considering the circumstances. I'll win them over one day."

And then break their hearts again when we get divorced. I didn't say it out loud because the night had already been hard enough.

Trevor hit the unlock button on his key fob and opened my door for me. "I appreciate you getting us out of there, but I do regret not getting one of your cupcakes. I still haven't had anything from your bakery. I'm not a very good husband."

"We can stop by and pick something up," I offered.

"Don't you need to get to work early?"

"No, I just said that, so we had an excuse to leave."

"Then, I would love to go." He leaned closer. "I'm going to kiss you now."

My eyes bugged out.

"We'll give Kelly a picture to send to my brother."

I laughed awkwardly. "Good idea. And thanks for the warning."

Bracing myself for being swept off my feet, I wasn't expecting Trevor to merely put his arm around my waist and plant a peck on my lips before letting go.

He opened the car door wider. "After you, wife."

———

When Tessa and I had plotted out our ideas for The Purrfect Café, we had decided right from the beginning that we didn't want to be open late. We had opted for a seven p.m. closing time during the week and nine p.m. on Friday and Saturday, and so far, it had worked well for us. Our busy hours were in the morning and early afternoon, and we had actually been talking about moving the time up but hadn't yet.

Thankfully, it was after eight, and The Purrfect Café was empty when Trevor and I walked in. I turned on the main lights and pulled a couple of chairs off a table for us to sit.

"What flavor of cupcake do you want?" I asked and pointed to the chalkboard behind the counter that listed everything we had.

"What's your favorite?"

"Tessa and her husband love lemon cupcakes. A lot of customers love the peanut butter ones. Cookies 'n' cream is pretty popular too. And then there is the salted caramel. Very popular. And there's red velvet."

"I didn't ask what everyone else's favorites were. I asked what yours was."

I also found my answer boring. "Chocolate. It's no fun, I know. Which is why I suggest—"

"I want chocolate."

"Are you sure?"

"Do they taste bad?"

I narrowed my eyes. "Of course not."

"Then, why are you second-guessing your favorite? I want chocolate."

I nodded and headed into the back. We cleared out the bakery case at night to store the cupcakes to keep them fresh. I pulled out two chocolate cupcakes and brought them out front.

Butterscotch, one of our café cats, was rubbing up against Trevor's leg.

"I forgot to make sure you were okay with cats."

He smiled. "Yes, I'm fine. I always wanted a pet, growing up, but my grandpa always said no."

I set his plate down. "But you own your own house now."

He shrugged. "It doesn't seem fair to an animal when I'm at work all day and I'm the only one who lives there." He smiled. "Or *was* the only one who lives there."

"It might not be fair to a dog, but a cat? They'd probably love it."

Picking up his cupcake and peeling the wrapper off, he said, "Good to know."

Butterscotch sat down and meowed.

"No. You can't have a cupcake," I told him and turned to watch Trevor take his first bite. For some reason, I was nervous he'd hate it.

Trevor closed his eyes and took a deep breath. He lifted his lids and looked at me. "This is almost better than sex."

"Almost?"

"Almost, but not quite."

"Hmph." I peeled off my own wrapper and took a bite. "I think chocolate cake is always better than sex."

"Then, you've been having the wrong kind of sex."

Chapter Fourteen

TREVOR

ALEXIS CAME HOME SATURDAY AFTERNOON, carrying a bakery box.

I met her at the door and kissed her. With Kelly Investigations watching us all the time, Alexis and I tried to do things a married couple would do, like greet each other.

Her lips were always soft, and there were times I was tempted to turn our pecks into something more, but I didn't want to cross a line and make her uncomfortable.

"What's this?" I asked her, lifting up the cover. So far, I loved everything she baked.

Slapping my hand away, she said, "I'm bringing my new grandmother-in-law cupcakes for dessert tonight."

I frowned. Not only was I not getting any treats, but I was also not looking forward to seeing my brother. It would have been hard enough to break the news of my marriage to my grandma without Kevin there. I had no idea how she was going to react.

"Your new but also former grandmother-in-law?"

"And that's why I'm bringing cupcakes. I might also need some sugar in case I need to stuff my face with food rather than stuff my fist in Kevin's face."

I stifled a laugh. "I think that's a wise idea. Kevin would probably charge you with assault. We can't give him the satisfaction."

"Very true. What time do we have to be there again?"

"Six, but I was thinking we should go early, so we can beat Kevin. That way, we can talk to Nana alone."

"Okay, let me take a quick shower first. I have flour all over me."

———

When Alexis and I pulled up to my grandmother's house, I was grateful to see that my brother had not arrived yet.

Alexis ran her hands back and forth on her bakery box. "How are we going to do this? Do you want to talk to her alone, and I can stay out here and wait until you're ready for me?"

I gave it careful consideration. My grandmother might take it better if I went in there alone, but what kind of husband would I be, leaving my wife in the car? And I wanted Nana to know we were a united front.

"No. I think you should come in with me."

"Let's do this then."

Alexis looked nervous as I took the bakery box in one hand and her palm in my other and led her to the front door. Normally, I would enter, knowing I was always welcome, but we were early, and I wasn't by myself.

"Ring the bell, please," I said and squeezed her hand. "It'll be okay. I promise."

She tried to smile, but it came out wobbly.

A second later, my grandma swung open the door. "Trevor. You're early," she said with a smile. Her eyes then glanced over at Alexis, and they widened. "Alexis. What are you doing here?"

"May we come in, Nana?" I asked.

She backed away, and we entered the house.

"I brought you these," Alexis said, and I handed over the cupcakes. "They're from my bakery."

Nana took the box, and her gaze went to where our hands were clasped together. She raised her eyebrows at me. "I think you have some explaining to do."

"Alexis and I got married."

She gasped, and her mouth fell. "You told me the last time we were together that there was no one special, and now, you're married? How could you do this to your brother?" She looked at Alexis. "Is this why my grandson left you? Because you were cheating on him with his brother?"

She turned back to me. "Is this why you lied about not dating anyone?"

"No, that's not what happened," I said.

Nana had already turned back to Alexis. "I thought you were better than this, young lady."

Alexis shrank into herself.

I stepped forward, putting Alexis behind me. "Enough."

"Oh, I have a few words for you too, young man. I can't believe you would—"

"I said, *enough*."

Nana took a step back. If she'd had pearls on, she would have been clutching them right now. "I can't believe you just spoke to me like that."

"Nana, I love you, but you are a little blind to your family. Alexis did not cheat on Kevin. She and I got together after their divorce was final. Kevin left because he wanted to, and their divorce was mutual. Neither of them fought it. It was what they both wanted." I wanted to tell her that Kevin had cheated on Alexis and that he owed her money, but I wasn't going to break her heart. "I'm not going to say any more, but you might not want to believe everything you hear." I reached behind me and pulled Alexis forward. "Now, if you would like to greet your new granddaughter-in-law, that would make me very happy."

Alexis spoke first. "I'm sorry, Mrs. Nelson. I told Trevor he should come in and talk to you alone."

Nana scoffed. "And leave his new wife outside on her own? I raised him better than that."

I smiled down at Alexis. "See? I told you."

Alexis smiled back, and Nana said, "Come on inside, and let's have a look at these cupcakes. Then, you can explain to me why I didn't get an invitation to your wedding."

We didn't get very far before the door swung open, and my brother walked in.

He gave me a fake smile when he saw me. "You're early, I see."

I looked at my watch. "So are you."

Nana immediately looked stressed as she glanced at her three guests. "Kevin, I think you should sit down. Your brother has some news for you."

Kevin waved Nana's concerns away. "I already know."

My grandmother looked like she was going to pass out from relief. "In that case, since you're here, we might as well sit down for dinner."

After we were all seated and our plates were full, my grandmother turned to Kevin. "I was expecting news tonight from you, not your brother. Did I get my wires crossed?"

"No, I also have an announcement."

"Oh? And what is that? I'm assuming it's not as big as Trevor's."

"Actually, Nana, I'm getting married."

Nana cupped her mouth. "This is wonderful news. Both my boys getting married before I'm gone."

I raised my glass to my lips and took a sip before I ruined my grandmother's good mood. "Where's the bride, Kevin?" I looked at Nana. "Have you even met her yet?"

"Now, Trevor, you sprang your marriage on me after the fact. I don't think you are in a place to judge." She turned to my brother. "But Trevor does have a point, Kevin. Where is this fiancée of yours?"

"She wanted to be here tonight—she really did—but she had to work."

"Bullshit," Alexis whispered for my ears only, and I agreed with her.

My brother didn't want Nana to see her very pregnant belly. I doubted Candace could even work in the United States yet.

"And the best part," my brother said, "is that you will get to come to the wedding."

Nana beamed at this news. "I can't wait," she said, but then her shoulders sagged. "When will the wedding be?"

My heart broke for her. She was worried she was going to miss it.

"Two weeks."

I sighed with relief. Even though my brother was a cheating bastard, I was grateful he was getting married soon enough for my grandmother to attend.

"I can't wait," Nana said.

"But that's not all." Kevin smiled, and I didn't like the cunning look in his eye. "Not only will you get to come to the wedding, but it will also take place in Florida."

"I love Florida," Nana said.

This was going better than I'd thought it would. Alexis and I wouldn't have to attend the wedding, and Nana was getting a trip.

"I know you do, and that's why I chose the destination. I wanted you to get one more vacation before..." Kevin looked down and sniffled.

My heart went out to my brother. Maybe he was more torn up about our grandmother being sick than I had thought he was. But then he looked up, his eyes clear and free of tears.

"As I was saying, I want you to get one more vacation, and that's why we're going to make it a family vacation. I rented a big place with three bedrooms, so we can spend the whole time together." He looked right at Alexis and me. "We won't be out of each other's sights."

Chapter Fifteen

ALEXIS

PANIC COURSED THROUGH MY BODY. *Vacation* was not the word I would use to describe spending time with my ex-husband and his pregnant fiancée; my grandmother-in-law, who didn't approve of me; and my fake husband, who I'd have to share a bed with, while we pretended to be a real couple twenty-four/seven. I didn't know if I could do it.

Then, there was the café.

"I can't just take off for however many days," I said. "I have a business to run."

Kevin smirked. "That's right. You opened a café and bakery. Who knew all that tinkering in the kitchen would lead to something?"

I clenched my jaw, and Trevor put his hand on my leg to try and calm me.

"Well, it did," I snapped back.

"How many days are you thinking?" Trevor's grandma asked.

"A week."

I shook my head. "Nope."

"Alexis," Trevor said, trying to get my attention.

I met his eyes. "I can't do that to Tessa."

He tilted his head toward the doorway. "Let's go talk in the other room."

I nodded in agreement.

We pushed back our chairs.

"We'll be right back," Trevor said and took my hand.

When we were clear of the dining room, he pulled me into a corner and put his hands on my hips. I could smell his cologne and see the flecks of gold in his dark brown eyes. My immediate thought was that I should pull away because we were too close. And because he felt too good.

I wondered what it would be like if I could touch him whenever I wanted. If I could put my arms around his shoulders. If I could run my nose along his neck. If I could kiss him there too.

Ugh. I needed to stop thinking sexual thoughts about my husband.

And that was a sentence one didn't hear every day.

"I know this is easier said than done, but please don't let Kevin get under your skin. That's what he wants," Trevor said.

"I know. He just knows exactly what buttons to push.

You know I quit my job for him, so I could stay home and be a mom. But when I didn't get pregnant, I started baking." At the time, it'd also made me feel like a failure. "He used to let me know that he liked what I made but that it was never quite good enough."

Trevor pulled me into his arms. "He's such a dick. I'm sorry he did that to you."

I closed my eyes and let myself enjoy his comfort for a few minutes.

"And listen"—his chest rumbled under my ear—"you absolutely do not have to go to Florida. We both know why Kevin is doing this, and we don't have to play into his hands."

I lifted my head. "What about you?"

"I will go. It might be Nana's last vacation, and I can't miss that."

"I can't let you go by yourself."

"I'll be fine. What's he going to do to me?"

"Piss you off until you snap his neck and go to prison?"

Trevor laughed. "Nah. He's not worth prison time."

I chewed on my lip. "What if he uses my absence at this family vacation as a reason to fight the will?"

"He can try, but it's last minute, and you really do have your business to take care of. No one can deny that."

I really wanted to let Trevor go by himself, but I also didn't want to do that to him. And I didn't want my ex to think he was right about our marriage situation.

"What if you and I didn't go for the whole week? Or I didn't go for the whole week? I can talk to Tessa. I'm sure I can manage a few days."

A smile spread across Trevor's face. "Are you sure?"

"Yeah. It's a few days. I'll survive."

He shook his head in wonder. "You are amazing. I could kiss you for this."

I knew he meant in a platonic way, but out of the corner of my eye, I saw Kevin headed our way.

"Kiss me then," I said in a normal tone. I dropped my voice. "Quick. Kevin's coming."

Trevor didn't need to be told twice.

He cupped the back of my neck and drew my mouth to his. His lips were soft, but I had expected that because I felt them every time he dropped a peck on my mouth. What I hadn't expected was for him to lick the seam of my lips and slide his way inside.

I moaned softly and clutched at his sides, trying to bring our bodies closer. It wasn't a surprise that Trevor was a great kisser, and all thoughts that this was all for show flew from my head.

Until Kevin cleared his throat.

Startled, I flinched and instinctively tried to jump back from Trevor like I was a teenager getting caught making out under the bleachers. But he yanked me closer and spun us around so that my back was to his chest and his arms were around me.

"What do you want, Kevin?" Trevor asked.

"Nana wants to know if you're coming on the trip or not." His eyes shifted down to me. "She's worried you're going to decline because of your new wife."

As if I had ever kept him from spending time with his family. I knew he was saying it just to piss me off, but it was working, and I wanted to punch the look right off his face.

Trevor squeezed me tighter. "That's ridiculous. Of course I'm going to go and spend time with my grandmother."

"What about Alexis?"

"Alexis is right here and can speak for herself," I said. "I can't come for the whole week, but I will come for a few days. I just need to clear it with Tessa."

Kevin curled his lip. "She never liked me."

I shrugged. "She has good taste."

Kevin's mouth pursed, and he looked like he was ready to shout profanities at me, but Trevor didn't let him get that far.

"Did you need anything else?"

My ex's chin went up. "Yeah. Why are there no chocolate cupcakes?"

"You brought out my cupcakes?"

"You brought them to eat, didn't you?"

I sighed. "Yes. And I brought more unique flavors tonight."

"I'd rather have chocolate," he muttered and walked away.

After he was gone, Trevor faced me again. "You didn't bring any chocolate? But it's your favorite?"

"It is, but it's also his. And I was feeling petty."

He threw his head back and laughed. Wrapping his arm around my neck, he led us back to the dining room. "Just bring some chocolate cupcakes home for the two of us next time," he whispered in my ear, and a shiver went down my spine as I remembered our kiss.

It was probably a good thing Kevin had interrupted us, but I sure wouldn't mind doing it again.

My life sucked. I had a sexy husband, and I couldn't even fuck him.

This whole thing had better work exactly as planned.

Chapter Sixteen

ALEXIS

I RUSHED into the restaurant to meet my friends the following Wednesday. I was running late and didn't want to miss out on any of the recent happenings in their lives. Although I was sure I was a big part of the latest gossip.

"Hey, ladies," I said, sliding into the one empty chair. "What did I miss?"

"Isabelle is single and officially a part of the United She-Woman Single Ladies with Our Vibrators So We Never Have Another Bad Date or Experience Romance Again Because Men Suck Club again," Tessa said.

I stuck out my lower lip. "I'm sorry, Isabelle."

"It's fine. I'm not that sad about it, which tells me it wasn't meant to be."

Elizabeth put her arm around Isabelle. "I'm glad I'm not the only single one anymore."

Pru cleared her throat. "Excuse me. I'm still very single."

"I'm glad Pru and I are not the only single ones anymore," Elizabeth corrected herself.

Pru nodded her thanks.

I raised my hand. "Uh...even though I'm technically married, I'm single too."

All eyes turned to me.

"How is that going, by the way?" Pru asked. "Is your new husband living up to his promises?"

"Actually, I met with a lawyer on Monday. He is going to file a motion for contempt of court."

Pru looked surprised, as did a few other friends.

"What happens then?" Bree asked.

"Kevin's going to be pissed," Paisley said.

"When does he find out you filed this?" Tessa asked, her eyes wide. She was the only one who knew about the trip to Florida.

"I'm waiting until after the trip," I told her. Then, I explained the vacation and wedding Kevin had planned. "I thought about not asking the attorney to wait because I'd love to see my ex pissed, but I don't want to ruin Trevor's grandma's last trip with her grandsons."

Bree nodded. "That's fair. Disappointing but fair."

"How's everything else going?" Pru asked.

"Have you boned yet?" Paisley spit out.

I snorted. "No. And we're not going to."

"Is that a trace of disappointment in your voice?" Paisley asked.

I straightened my spine. "*No.*" A second later, I slumped in my seat. "Maybe. Even though it would complicate everything."

"He is your husband. Why not have sex?" Isabelle asked.

"I literally just said, it would complicate everything."

She shrugged. "It's already complicated. He's your ex-husband's brother."

I looked down at my hands. "He doesn't think of me like that."

"You don't know that," Tessa said in a soft voice.

"I've never said anything about this, but when I met Trevor and Kevin, Trevor was the one I liked right away."

Tessa gasped. "You never told us that."

"That's because it's embarrassing when you like someone and they don't like you back. Plus, by the time that trip was over, I had already gotten Kevin's number and was coming around to him."

I had met the brothers on a summer trip with my family, where my parents had rented a cabin. I had almost not gone because I was in college and too cool for stuff like that. At the time, I was glad I had gone because I'd met Trevor and Kevin, but now, I wondered what would have happened had I not gone.

"Wait," Pru said. "You always told us that you met

Kevin when he was skinny-dipping. Was Trevor there too?"

I smiled and nodded. "It was the first and last time I saw my husband naked." I laughed because there was no other way to react. "And that's how it's going to stay." I sighed. "But pretending to be in love and touching each other at Kevin's wedding? It's going to be torture. He kissed me last weekend when Kevin was walking into the room. I had to go home and break out my vibrator."

Paisley leaned in. "I think you should just ask him to have sex. Get the first time over with. Then, you can have sex on the trip, loud enough for Kevin to hear."

I pictured the steam coming out of my ex's ears. "Tempting, but it's one thing to kiss and do PDA. It's another to have sex for a fake relationship." I didn't think my ego could handle Trevor having sex with me just to prove we were a real couple. It wouldn't sit well with me.

"I'm sure Trevor would love to have sex with you for more than just this situation you two have going on. He did ask you to be his wife. I bet there's a reason he asked you and no one else," Paisley continued.

Hmm. I hadn't thought about it like that.

"Do you really think he's interested in me? Even if it's just a little bit?"

"Definitely," Paisley said.

"I'm not sure if I can trust your opinion. You're newly in love with Colin." She gasped, but I looked at

Pru. "You were at our marriage ceremony. What do you think?"

I also know Pru would give it to me straight.

"I think Paisley might be onto something." She lifted her shoulders. "You never know unless you try."

"Yeah," Bree said. "Also, we need to meet this husband of yours."

I wrinkled my nose. "You all have before. He was in my wedding to Kevin. I think a few of you danced with him at the reception."

"We need to meet him again as your husband," Elizabeth said.

"I'll see what I can do."

———

That night, when I got home, I went to find Trevor.

He was in his office on his laptop.

"Hey," I said.

He glanced up at me before looking back at his computer. "Hey. How was dinner?"

"Good."

"Was the investigator there?" he asked, not looking up.

Picking up a pen on his desk, I said, "Yeah. I hope he was bored."

"What did your friends say about him?"

"I didn't tell them."

He looked up at me with raised eyebrows.

"I didn't want to freak them out. I'll tell them when this whole thing is over and Kevin is out of my life."

"Hmm." He turned back to his screen, leaving me to wonder what his response meant.

Could he not want our marriage to end? Could Paisley be right?

I sat on the corner of the desk. I'd worn a casual dress to dinner, and I made sure the hem of the skirt shifted up my leg to show a little skin.

"Do you think I made the wrong decision?" I asked.

Trevor scanned my face, down my leg, back up to my face, and shrugged. "They're your friends. You know them best." He pointed to his laptop. "I don't want to be rude, but I need to finish what I'm working on."

Heat filled my cheeks, and I scrambled off his desk.

Paisley was oh-so wrong.

"Sorry. I didn't mean to bother you," I said, heading for the door.

"You're not bothering—"

"Have a good night."

As I got ready for bed and shut myself in my bedroom, I had to wonder if revenge was worth my self-respect.

Chapter Seventeen

TREVOR

"ARE you sure you'll be okay, going to Florida on your own?" I asked Alexis.

We were just getting to the airport, where I was meeting my grandmother, my brother, and his fiancée. Alexis was coming four days later to spend three days in Florida, and then we were coming back to Minnesota at the end of the week together.

"I'm a big girl, Trevor. I can even travel all by myself."

"I appreciate the sarcasm, but I'm serious. You don't have to come if it's too much for you."

She pulled up to the curb and put her car in park. She turned in her seat. "Are you going to meet me at the airport when I get there?"

"Of course."

"Then, I'll be there."

"Just know, if you change your mind or if something

comes up, I won't hold it against you. This trip wasn't part of our arrangement."

She put her hand on my arm. "I appreciate it, but I'll be fine. It'll be a good way to prove to Kevin that we're in this together."

I smiled. Our marriage might be fake and for reasons that didn't involve love, but we were in it together. That was one hundred percent true.

And it made me want to kiss her again.

I'd been wanting to since the day my brother had announced his destination wedding. I couldn't stop thinking about how good she had felt and the way she'd responded to me.

I'd had to relieve myself every day since then—and twice on the day she'd come home from her dinner with her friends.

When she'd sat on my desk, I had wanted to pull her over my lap and onto my cock. I was so hard, and all I could think about was her riding me until both of us came. But I was sure she didn't realize what she was doing, and when I'd asked her to leave, I'd felt so guilty. Even if it was the right decision.

"Trevor?"

I looked at Alexis.

"Are you okay? You seemed to be lost in your thoughts."

"I'm okay." Just hard and horny again.

"You know, you don't have to go either."

I smiled. "I know. I'll be fine. That's not what's bothering me."

"Oh no. What's bothering—"

Drawing her toward me, I kissed her.

Her lips parted for me, and I sucked on the bottom one before I slid my tongue inside. She tasted just like she had the last time I kissed her, and I wished I could do this every day. And then some. My dick ached to the point that it was going to be difficult to walk into the airport.

A horn honked off in the distance, and I reluctantly pulled away.

"I'm sorry. I thought I saw my brother out there," I lied. "It seemed reasonable we'd kiss good-bye."

She licked her lips, and my crotch tightened. I wanted to take her mouth again. I wanted her to do that to my dick.

It was a good thing I was leaving town.

"I'd better get going. I promised Nana I'd meet her inside."

"I wish she had let us bring her to the airport."

I swung open my car door. "Me too, but she insisted her neighbor could drive her." I got out of the vehicle and leaned over, so I could see Alexis's face. "Remember to act like you missed me when you get to Florida."

She smiled, a small glint in her eye. "But I will miss you."

"You know what I mean. Act like you missed your newlywed husband."

"Got it. Be prepared to catch me."

I laughed, having no idea what she was referring to. "See you in a few days."

"See you then."

I closed the door, grabbed my luggage from the trunk, and headed inside the airport. As I neared the location where we had all agreed to meet, I saw my grandma already standing there.

"Nana." I waved my hand in the air.

When I reached her, she was smiling, which meant my brother and his fiancée probably weren't there yet.

"Hi, Nana," I said, giving her a hug.

"Hello, dear."

"Have you seen Kevin yet?"

"No, and I'm getting awfully anxious."

"Don't you think it's odd that he hasn't introduced his fiancée to you yet? And now, he's getting married this week?"

She looked me up and down in the only way a matriarch would. "Says the man who didn't introduce his wife to me until after he was married."

"Touché," I agreed. "Except you already knew Alexis."

"Still counts, young man."

"Got it."

"Where is that new wife of yours anyway?"

I looked over Nana in concern. She was elderly, but she still had a good memory. "She's coming in a few days. Remember? She has a business she can't leave for a week."

"That's right. The cupcakes."

"It's actually a café and bakery," I explained. "A cat café."

"What is a cat café?"

"It's a café with cats that you can pet and adopt."

She raised her eyebrows. "Seems like a way to introduce germs into the food."

My shoulders slumped. "The cats aren't allowed in the kitchen, and the customers love it."

"If you say so."

I sighed. Getting her to accept Alexis was going to be harder than I'd thought it would be.

"Oh, there's your brother," Nana said, and I looked in the direction she was facing.

Sure enough, there was Kevin with a pregnant Candace trailing behind him.

As he got closer, Nana said, "Where's his fiancée?"

I could see how she would have trouble with all the people walking toward us and with Candace behind him, but I thought it seemed obvious they were together. Plus, Nana had met Candace when she was living with Alexis and Kevin.

When my brother reached us, he gave our grandmother a hug and held out his arm. "Nana, do you remember Candace?"

Candace stepped forward, and Kevin put his arm around her.

"Candace, this is my grandmother. You can call her Nana."

Nana straightened her spine and lifted her nose. "She can call me Mrs. Nelson."

I winced. I'd known this introduction wouldn't go well, but I felt bad for the young woman. Kevin, not so much. He deserved it. Even when he had been married to Alexis and Nana liked her, Alexis always called our grandma by her first name.

"Nana, I don't think that's fair to my fiancée."

"I don't think it's fair that you didn't tell me you got someone pregnant and are only now marrying her." She scanned Candace. "Are you even allowed to go on the airplane?"

I hadn't even thought of that. Candace looked like she was going to give birth.

She swallowed and glanced at Kevin before answering, "I'm only thirty weeks. I can fly up to thirty-six," she said quietly.

Nana narrowed her eyes and clenched her jaw. "That is, if we even get on this flight at all."

Chapter Eighteen

ALEXIS

I HAD JUST FINISHED MIXING up batter for another batch of cupcakes when my phone buzzed in my pocket. I was making extra batches to keep in the fridge, so they only had to be baked while I was out of town.

> Trevor: I made it to Florida. Barely. Nana almost called off the trip.

I laughed.

> Me: No way.

> Trevor: Oh yeah. She was pissed at Kevin when she saw Candace.

> Me: To be fair, I would be mad too.

The woman had lost her husband and her only child,

and her two grandsons had just sprung marriages on her. It wasn't any wonder she wasn't impressed with them right now.

> Trevor: I found something out. Not sure it matters though.

> Me: What's that?

I was expecting some juicy gossip, but that wasn't what I got.

> Trevor: Candace is only 30 weeks pregnant, which puts her at just over seven months. I know it probably means that Kevin still cheated on you because who knows how long they were sleeping together before she got pregnant, but I thought you should know he might have waited until you were divorced.

That was really sweet of Trevor to try and make me feel better. Kevin and I had been divorced for nine months, so it could be possible that they'd slept together after that. But that wasn't what really bothered me. After all, Candace could gladly have him.

Me: Thank you, but I don't really care so much on whether he may or may not have cheated. Our marriage was over before we even separated. They're welcome to each other. But I don't think it's fair they get to have a baby, and I don't.

Trevor: I agree. It should have been you.

Me: Thank you. Anyway, I'm thinking about taking home one of the cats from work. Once I get a bigger place of my own, that is.

I'd made sure to add the last line, so he didn't think I was going to bring a cat to his house.

Trevor: Which cat?

Me: I actually have a couple I love. There's the black-and-white cat. His name is Salt and Pepper. And then there is the orange cat named...wait for it...Ginger.

Trevor: So original.

I laughed as the door to the kitchen opened. But I didn't look up, as I was too busy texting Trevor back.

Me: We're a café and bakery. We had to name her Ginger.

Trevor: There are a ton of orange foods.
Mangoes, apricots, peaches, carrots,
sweet potatoes, and...wait for
it...oranges.

I laughed again.

Me: Orange? Boring.

"Whatcha doing?"

I jumped and slapped my hand over my chest. "You scared me."

Tessa chuckled as she came closer. "Sorry."

"No, you're not."

"Okay, maybe I'm only a little sorry." She nodded to my phone. "So, what are you doing?"

"Texting Trevor. Why?"

"Because you have a huge smile on your face."

I knew what she was getting at, but I refused to consider it. "He just told me that his grandma almost called off the trip because she was upset with Kevin. She had no idea he had gotten someone pregnant. How could I not smile?"

Tessa gave me a side-eye look.

"Stop it."

She lifted her hands up. "Stop what?"

"Thinking what you're thinking."

She grinned. "And what am I thinking?"

I pointed my finger at her. "I don't know. Just stop it."

"How about I tell you what I'm thinking?"

"I'm all ears." But I wasn't. I was afraid of what she was going to say.

"I think you should go to Florida tomorrow."

My eyebrows flew up. That was not what I had expected her to say.

"I can't do that." I looked around the kitchen. "There's too much to do. I can't leave you hanging like that."

Tessa walked over to our main fridge and opened it. She pointed inside to the numerous storage containers of batter in there. "I think I'll be fine."

I shook my head. "I'm not sure it's enough."

She shrugged. "So what? We run out of some stuff? It will only make people appreciate it more."

"I don't know about that."

She reached into her back pocket and pulled out her phone. She pushed a few buttons and handed it to me. "Read."

With a sigh, I looked at her screen.

> Tessa: Hey, handsome.

> Seth: Hey, beautiful.

> Tessa: Question for you.

> Seth: Yes, I will make you come when I get home tonight.

> Tessa: LOL. No. I have a question for the advertiser, not my husband.

Seth: Bummer. What's the question?

> Tessa: Alexis might go to Florida early. If we run out of baked goods toward the end, will it hurt our business?

Seth: If you run out the day before she gets back and it doesn't happen again, it might help. Customers would realize what it's like not to get your products. They might appreciate your food more. But if it happens repeatedly, they might stop coming in.

> Tessa: Great. Thank you!

Seth: You're welcome.

> Tessa: As for the first answer you gave me...I'll make sure Alexis makes extra lemon frosting before she leaves.

Seth: Can't wait. I'm going to—

"And that's where I stop." I quickly handed her cell back to her before I read more of what was for her eyes only. "You could have warned me there was sexy talk on there."

"Pfft. You're fine. Besides, you saw what you needed to see, right?"

I sighed. "Yes."

"Good." She headed for the front of the bakery. "Just think about it."

I stared at the door swinging back and forth after she walked out. I did kind of miss Trevor, but could I really be around Kevin and Candace for that many days?

My phone vibrated on the counter.

Trevor: Check out this view.

He sent a video. It showed the inside of the house in Florida. It was decorated beautifully, and it looked exactly how I pictured a Florida beach home to look with accent walls of white wood siding. Trevor stepped outside, where there was a pool off to one side, but right behind the house was the beach and the ocean.

Trevor: Wish you were here.

Me: Can you come and pick me up at the airport tomorrow?

Chapter Nineteen

TREVOR

I CHECKED the arrival time on the board at the airport. Alexis's flight had landed five minutes early. I just had to wait for her to make it to baggage claim.

"How much longer?" Kevin whined.

"Please stop. You're the one who insisted on coming with me."

"Yeah, but I thought you were going to just pull the rental car in front and have her get in. I didn't know you were going to come inside."

I turned to him. "You're more than welcome to go out to the parking lot and wait."

He crossed his arms over his chest. "No, I'll stay."

"Then, please stop complaining."

I wasn't sure why my brother had insisted on accompanying me. I didn't know if he needed a break from Nana's judging looks or if he wanted to keep an eye on Alexis and me since his little spy wouldn't have followed us across the country. Either way, he was getting on my nerves.

More people started heading toward baggage claim, and I forgot all about my brother as I kept my eyes open for my wife.

It wasn't long, although it felt like too much time had passed until I saw her face. Her hair was pulled up in a messy bun, and she wasn't wearing makeup, but she looked beautiful. When she saw me, she grinned and started running toward me.

I held out my arms, and right before she reached me, she jumped into them. She wrapped her arms and legs around me and hugged me tight.

I hadn't told her Kevin was coming with me, and I wasn't sure if she had seen him, but I loved that she'd stepped into wife mode right away.

She released me, and I set her down, kissing her just enough for her to know I was glad to see her.

"How was your flight?"

"Good."

I put my arm around her neck and kissed her forehead. "Great. Let's go get your luggage, shall we?"

As we turned, we almost ran into my brother.

"Oh," Alexis said, jumping back. "I didn't realize you came."

Either she was the world's best actress or she really

hadn't known, and I felt my chest swell with her reaction to seeing me again.

"I couldn't get him to stay home," I told her.

"It's fine. We're going to be sharing a place for almost a week. I might as well get used to having him around."

"Stop talking like I'm not here." Kevin sneered. "You used to live with me year-round."

Alexis raised her eyebrows. "Don't judge me for my past mistakes."

I laughed, and the two of us continued to the baggage carousel.

————

"Our place is within walking distance of restaurants, cafés, shops, and the beach," I told Alexis as I drove us back to our rental place. I had to admit that Kevin had done a good job on picking a location. "When Nana found out you were coming, she suggested we all go to dinner together. Does that work for you?"

"I'm here to spend time with your family. I'll do whatever," she said from the backseat. She had been nice enough not to argue with Kevin on who got shotgun.

Despite her relaxed demeanor at the airport and in the car, she grew tense when we got back to the house. I thought maybe she was worried about my grandmother, but when Candace walked into the room, Alexis stiffened completely.

Candace stopped in her tracks and smiled when she saw Alexis. "Alexis, I thought you were coming in a few days."

Candace rushed forward, and Alexis moved closer to me, but that didn't stop Candace from pulling Alexis in for a hug.

Alexis's arms hung at her sides, and I didn't understand how Candace was so clueless to Alexis's body language.

"I'll show you to our bedroom," I said, rescuing her. "Then, you can unpack before we go to dinner."

Candace stepped back, and I quickly took Alexis's hand, grabbed her suitcase, and showed her to our room.

The house we were renting was compact. It had one large open space with the kitchen, dining, and living area. There was a front door facing the street and a patio door in the back. Adjacent to those were two bedrooms on one side and a bedroom and bathroom on the other.

"We're over here," I said. "The location is great, but the place is small." I pointed to the bedroom next to us. "That's where Kevin and Candace are staying." And I pointed to the other side of the main area. "That's Nana's room and the bathroom. We thought she should be the closest to it. Sorry, that puts us next to Kevin and Candace."

"It's fine. My discomfort takes a backseat to an elderly woman." She looked around. "Where is your grandma?"

"Probably napping." I cleared my throat. "I guess she's been more tired lately." Sometimes, I forgot that Nana had cancer, but this trip had reminded me in a big way.

"I'm sorry, Trevor."

I smiled. "Not your fault." I didn't want to think about it. "Let's get you unpacked."

We entered our room, and I shut the door, so we could talk privately.

I set her suitcase on the bed. "There's a closet and dresser in here if you don't want to leave your stuff in your bag."

"Thanks."

"But the bed is only a queen." I lowered my voice just in case Kevin decided to eavesdrop. "If you want to put something between us while we sleep, I can find an extra pillow."

She put her hand up to stop me. "We're adults. I'm sure we can manage."

I smiled.

After the first night when Kevin had burst in, I'd had the locks changed, and she'd been staying in her own room every night. I was looking forward to sleeping next to my wife while we were here. I didn't know what that meant, but I was sure it was harmless.

As Alexis unpacked her clothes, I sat on the bed and leaned against the headboard.

"Are you just going to watch me?" she asked.

I shrugged. "Why not?"

"Because it's boring."

"Not to me." I liked spending time with her.

"Thanks for intervening out there with Candace."

I frowned. "I'm sorry she approached you like that."

Candace had acted like she and Alexis were best friends.

"It is weird. The last time I saw her was at a restaurant with Kevin. She knew I was upset, and I refused to talk to her. Now, she's acting like nothing is wrong."

"Maybe because you're here, she thinks everything is good between the two of you."

She seemed to consider this. "You might be right. And honestly, I don't want to stay mad at her. She can have Kevin. I just feel betrayed. I thought we were friends. Even if divorced, friends don't date each other's exes. At least, not without talking to each other first." She took a deep breath. "But my biggest problem with Candace is my own." She turned and sat on the bed. "I'm jealous that she's pregnant when I couldn't be. And I'm so damn pissed that Kevin gets to have a baby, and I don't."

I scooted forward and put her bag on the floor. Moving next to her, I put my arm around her and pulled her to me. "I'm sorry, Alexis. Life is nothing but unfair sometimes."

Chapter Twenty

ALEXIS

DINNER WAS a little tense at first. The five of us stared at each other while the waitress took our drink orders.

Trevor and I had walked down to the restaurant early. I thought a drink or two might loosen me up enough to eat with Kevin and Candace. Kevin had driven down with his grandma and Candace. It was too far for an elderly woman with cancer and an expectant mother to walk.

Thankfully, the two mojitos I'd had before the rest of our dinner party got there was enough to loosen me up for small talk.

We were at a table with Candace and me across from each other, Trevor and Kevin across from each other, and their grandmother at the end, between her grandsons.

I looked at Trevor's grandma. "Are you excited to meet your great-grandchild?"

The surprise that sprang on the woman's face had me wondering if she had never thought about it.

"Yeah, Nana," Kevin said, putting his arm around Candace. "We don't know what we're having yet, but we were thinking if it's a boy, we'd name him after Grandpa."

Candace frowned for a moment but then forced a smile on her face. "We're still talking about it, but it's in the running."

I lifted my newest drink to my lips and sipped. It seemed Candace wasn't on board with naming the baby after her fiancé's grandfather.

"As it should be. William is a strong name," Nana said. She cleared her throat and relaxed her stance. "How has your pregnancy been?"

Candace rubbed her belly. "Good. I was sick in the beginning, but that went away months ago."

"I was sick with Kevin and Trevor's father."

Trevor leaned closer to me and whispered in my ear, "Was this your goal? To get Nana to like Candace?"

"Maybe," I whispered back. "A great-grandmother deserves to know her great-grandchild before she passes. And the baby is innocent in all this."

Trevor put his arm around me. "You're a good person."

I snorted. "I'm an okay person."

He grinned and kissed me. It wasn't very sexual, but when we separated, Kevin was staring at us. I met his eyes and took another sip of my mojito.

Kevin put his hand on Candace's belly. "Would you like to feel the baby move, Nana?"

I shifted in my seat, trying not to let my jealousy at that question consume me.

"Yes, Mrs. Nelson, you have to feel the baby move." Candace looked at me. "Would you like to feel too, Alexis? He's kicking right now."

It seemed like she was trying to be nice, but it felt like a kick to the gut. "No, thank you."

Kevin stood. "Switch seats with me," he said to Candace.

She took Kevin's seat and placed his grandmother's hand on her belly.

We all sat, waiting for a few seconds until Candace's face lit up and Nana smiled.

"Did you feel that?" Candace asked.

"I did," Nana said. She took her hand away. "I'm sorry I was short with you at the airport. I wasn't happy to find out Kevin had kept you from me and waited so long to marry you."

"Nana, I told you, we needed to get her back into the country before we could get married."

"You still could have told me before."

Kevin pursed his lips but said, "You're right."

"Either way, there's no reason I can't enjoy my great-grandchild even if it's only for a short time," Nana said. She smiled, but it was sad. "If I make it until then."

Trevor took her hand. "You will, Nana. I have faith."

"Thank you." She turned back to Candace. "At least I have the opportunity, right? I thought Alexis would give me grandchildren, but that didn't happen."

Immediately, I looked back and forth between Kevin and his grandmother. *What did he tell her?*

"Alexis had talked about it, but I guess she was too busy to make it happen."

Candace gasped, and Trevor whispered, "*Nana.*"

I didn't really think that her words were meant to hurt me, but hurt me they did.

Reaching behind me, I removed Trevor's arm from my shoulders. I pushed back my chair. "Please excuse me. I'm not feeling well. I think I'm going to head back to the house." I stood and looked in Trevor's direction, but I couldn't meet his eyes. "Do you have the key?"

He pushed his chair back also. "I'll come with you."

I stopped him with my hand. "No, you stay and have dinner."

He lifted my chin. "I'm coming with."

Putting my hand on his arm, I said, "You don't have much time left with your grandmother. Please. Stay."

His jaw clenched.

"I want to be alone for a bit anyway, and it will make me feel better if you stay."

Trevor reached into his pocket and pulled out the key.

I swiped it from him. "See you after dinner."

I headed out of the restaurant and tried to keep my wits about me until I got back to the rental. When I got there, it took several tries for me to get the key in the lock, which was when the tears started to fall.

Finally, I got the door open, and I quickly slammed it shut and sprinted to our room. I threw the bedroom door closed, too, and collapsed on the bed as I started to sob.

I hated that my body had failed me in that aspect. And I hated even more that it meant so much to me. Why couldn't I be one of those women who never wanted kids?

I didn't know how long I'd been lying there, but I heard the click of the bedroom door opening. I kept my back turned, figuring it was Trevor. Not wanting him to know how upset I was, I tried to silence my tears.

But when he lay beside me and pulled me into his arms, I turned and cried into his chest. It felt so good to be held. I didn't care anymore if he saw me at my worst.

———

I woke up the next morning, still fully clothed, on top of the covers and in Trevor's arms. I carefully pushed myself up so as not to wake him.

His eyes were closed, and his mouth was partially open. He looked quite adorable. With his dark hair and dark eyes, he was so masculine, but seeing him sleep made him a little more boyish.

I must have stared too long because he groaned and rolled onto his back.

He smacked his tongue against the roof of his mouth. "Ugh, I need to brush my teeth."

I chuckled. "Same. I didn't wash my face either."

He reached out and put his hand on my hip. "You still look beautiful."

"Ha. Thank you, but I hate the feeling of not getting ready for bed."

Stretching as he sat up, he said, "I haven't fallen asleep without my nightly routine in years. It wasn't even late. I must be getting old."

I hit my shoulder against his and got off the bed before he caught a whiff of my morning breath. "Sorry about last night. I didn't mean to ruin dinner."

"My grandmother ruined dinner."

"Did you at least get to eat something?" I had no idea how long I had lain in bed before Trevor got home.

His stomach answered by growling.

"That would be a no," he said.

"How about we shower and go find some breakfast? Just the two of us?"

"Sounds like a plan."

"Do you want to shower first or last?" *Or we could save time and shower together?*

And that was not a thought I should be having this

morning. Just because I'd slept in the comfort of his arms didn't mean he wanted to have sex.

"You go first."

Quickly, I grabbed my clothes and left the bedroom before I made things more complicated.

I was nearly to the bathroom when Trevor's grandma's door opened, and we almost ran into each other.

I stepped back. "Go ahead."

"I'll only be a minute," she said.

I smiled politely. "No worries."

Nana went in and used the toilet and washed her hands. When she came out, I tried to duck inside, but she stopped me.

"Alexis?"

"Yes?"

"I apologize for last night. Trevor explained to me about your...troubles and that I was quick to judge."

Hearing that Trevor had done that warmed my heart.

"Thank you for apologizing."

Nana looked down at her feet. "Even though I had Trevor's father, we were never able to have another child. I know it's not quite the same, but I do understand your pain."

"I'm sorry to hear that."

She looked up at me. "Thank you, dear."

We stood for a few moments before I said, "I'd better get in the shower. Trevor and I are going to breakfast."

She moved out of the way. "Yes, yes, of course."

She headed toward her bedroom.

"Mrs. Nelson?"

She turned.

"Would you like to join Trevor and me?"

She smiled. "No, dear. You go and enjoy some time with your husband."

"Will do."

"And, Alexis?"

"Yes?"

"You can call me Adele."

Chapter Twenty-One

ALEXIS

BREAKFAST WAS DELICIOUS. Trevor and I were both so hungry that we hardly said anything to each other as we stuffed our faces.

After we got back to the house, we all voted to go to the beach.

"You sure you're up for that?" Trevor asked.

I loved that he was worried about me.

"Yes. Last night was therapeutic, and I don't want to waste the beautiful weather being sad. Especially when it won't change anything."

He grinned. "Let's go then."

The best part of the rental was having the beach practically in the backyard. The house also came with huge beach towels, beach chairs, and plenty of sunblock to cover us each ten times over. There were some umbrellas so that Adele and anyone else could sit in the shade.

"I was thinking we could grill something for dinner," Trevor said as we set up.

"I'm in," I said. I did not want to have to worry about showering again just to go eat.

I laid my towel over my chair and took off my cover-up.

I heard Trevor make a noise behind me, and I spun around to see what was wrong. He was laying his own towel out. He must have been fighting with it.

I pulled out the strongest sunscreen there was because I was all about sun safety, and I put it on my arms, legs, stomach, and face.

"Do you need me to get your back?" Trevor's deep voice said behind me.

"Yes, please," I said and handed the bottle to him. I put my head down so he could get my neck and waited.

His hands were large and warm, and he didn't rush putting the sunblock on me. He made sure to get every inch of exposed skin and massaged it into me thoroughly. Even though I had gotten my front, with the cut of my two-piece, he was grazing my sides. My nipples peaked, as if to say they wanted to be touched, and I had to hold back a moan.

I had been with one guy after my divorce, mostly so Kevin wouldn't be the last guy I had slept with, but it hadn't been anything special. I hadn't had great sex in a long time, and my body was protesting.

Trevor finished my upper back and moved to the lower

half. I was both disappointed and relieved. The bottom part didn't feel nearly as sexy—until he got to the outside of my hips. I closed my eyes and imagined him pulling me back against his body with one hand as the other slipped beneath the bottoms and over my pussy.

My clit practically throbbed, and this time, there was no holding back my moan.

Trevor immediately stopped. "Are you okay?"

Just hornier than I ever have been in my life.

"Yep." I stepped forward and turned, putting a bright smile on my face so he wouldn't sense my embarrassment. "Your turn."

He chuckled. "I don't use sunscreen."

I gasped.

"I don't burn."

Trevor's mother had been from South America, and he had gotten her tan skin tone, so I believed him when he said he didn't burn.

"That's no excuse. Everyone should use sunscreen. Everyone. Just ask any dermatologist."

He rolled his eyes but handed me the bottle and swung around. "Get my back for me?" he asked, pulling off his shirt.

I swallowed. I had seen my husband shirtless since we'd gotten married, but besides our PDA experiment, I hadn't touched him. His back was strong and his shoulders broad. I wanted to kiss his spine between his shoulder blades, not put sunscreen on him.

Pull yourself together, Alexis.

I managed to spread the sunblock on him only because I looked at Kevin the whole time. My ex was enough to smother some of the flames in my body. Except I was so set on not focusing on Trevor that I missed him twisting so that his front was facing me now.

"Oh."

His chest was muscular with a sprinkling of dark hair and right in front of my face.

"If you want me to wear sunblock, you have to put it on me."

I knew he was teasing me because I was the one who was making him wear it, but this was just torture now. And it would look really weird if he saw me watching my ex-husband.

I was going to have to do this quick. I squeezed the bottle so hard that I got way more sunscreen in my hand than I needed, but at least I wouldn't have to go back for more.

Slapping my hands down on his shoulders, I hastily spread the lotion everywhere as quickly as I could, but it didn't help. As I touched him, his muscles flexed exactly the way I pictured they would if I caressed him while we were naked.

I couldn't do it anymore.

I jumped back. "You'll have to do your legs." No way was I bending down in front of him. I couldn't guarantee I wouldn't do anything outrageous if his dick was *right there*.

Trevor looked down at the white streaks I'd left on him.

"Sorry," I muttered. "It's an emergency. I'll be right back." I spun on my heel and ran for the house, fully aware that I probably gave the impression that my emergency was bathroom-related.

But it was better than him knowing the truth.

I made it to our bedroom and my suitcase. I had unpacked most things, except my special friend I'd traveled with. I unzipped the small pocket inside my bag and pulled out my G-spot vibrator. It was long and curved and hit the spot perfectly. But it also worked great on my clit, too, when I wanted something different.

I had never been so aroused that I had to leave a family gathering to masturbate, but I could be embarrassed later. Right now, I needed an orgasm. Maybe two. I needed one at least to take the edge off.

I shut the bedroom door and hit the lock button on the knob. It wouldn't stay in.

"*Dammit.*" I tried it a couple more times, making sure the door was shut before giving up. "Fuck it."

The house was silent with only the sound of the over-head fans creating a low hum. I'd be able to hear someone walking in the house.

I kicked off my bottoms and my top. Even though my clit was what was going to get me to my destination, my nipples wanted to be part of the ride. They were still hard from earlier.

I fell back onto the bed and got comfortable before turning my vibrator on.

Chapter Twenty-Two

ALEXIS

CLOSING MY EYES, I touched my vibrator on the top of my mons. I knew I wasn't going to last long, and I wanted to tease myself just a little. I trailed the toy from one side of my lips to the other as I used my other hand to pinch my nipple. I hadn't even put it inside me yet, and I was already so wet.

When I felt something on my thigh, I thought I had imagined it. But when I opened my eyes, I saw Trevor standing there, and I sucked in a breath.

I wasn't sure what to do, but it seemed he did.

Trevor sat on the bed and took the vibrator from my hand. I spread my legs wide and almost came just from the anticipation.

I had no idea how long he'd been watching me, but he picked up where I'd left off. He ran my vibrator over my pussy, but he skipped the good parts. It felt like forever. It didn't feel long enough. But by the time he pushed it slowly inside me, I moaned long and hard.

He fucked me a few times with the toy before pulling it out to rub it on my clit.

My pelvis arched in the air at the sudden stimulation. It was almost too much to bear. I was grinding my hips, getting closer to coming when Trevor pulled his hand away.

I cried out as he crawled onto the bed and lay on his stomach, and then I could do nothing but stare at him. Looking into my eyes, he pushed the toy inside me again, followed by him putting his mouth right on my swollen nub.

My eyes rolled to the back of my head, and I hadn't even orgasmed yet. The pleasure was so intense that I knew that when I blew, it was going to be epic.

And suddenly, I realized that wasn't what I wanted.

I popped open my eyes and sat up. Trevor straightened, questions in his eyes.

His swim trunks were tight across his crotch, and I brushed my hand over his hard dick. I slid my hand into his trunks and took him in my fist. He was warm and thick in my hand.

"I don't want a sex toy in me when I come. I want you."

Trevor closed his eyes.

I knew there was a risk he might reject me because he'd never shown interest in me before, but I figured I had a good shot at him saying yes after he'd just gone down on me. But for a moment, I was second-guessing my boldness.

I started to let go, and he clamped his hand around mine.

His lids slowly lifted. "I don't have a rubber."

I grinned. That was a problem I could work with.

"Do you have anything you don't want to give me?"

"No."

"Same goes for me. And since I can't get pregnant..." I moved onto my knees and put my mouth next to his ear. "Besides, if you can't fuck your wife without a condom, who can you?"

He groaned. "Fuck. When you put it like that, who am I to argue?" Grinning, he nudged me until I fell on my back.

I laughed at first until he pushed his swim trunks off. I sighed at the sight of him and licked my lips.

His cock was beautiful.

"I want to taste it," I blurted out.

"Later," he said, positioning himself between my thighs. "I don't know when someone else is going to come in the house, and I would really hate to be interrupted." He brushed his shaft over my pussy, coating himself in my desire. "So wet," he said under his breath to himself.

"Good—"

Trevor pushed himself inside me.

"Point." I sucked in a breath and clenched the bedding in my hands. "*Holy shit*," I panted.

He licked his thumb and rubbed my clit. "Are you okay?"

"No."

An eyebrow went up, and his thumb froze. "No?"

"No. But in the best possible way. It's been a while since I've had sex, and I need a moment to adjust to your size." I grinned.

"That's a pretty good problem to have, I guess." He pushed his thumb down into my wetness and back up to my clit. "But I'd better make sure you feel more than just good."

I tightened around him as he circled my nub, and he began to rock back and forth, shallow at first.

But it wasn't long before I adjusted to his size. I cupped my breasts in my hands and pinched my nipples. "Oh God. Oh, yes. I'm so close. Please, please, please, I need to come."

As I was right on the edge, Trevor took my hands in his, shoving them above my head as he drove into me. His cock hit my G-spot as his pubis did the same with my clit.

My orgasm slammed into me. My whole body tightened as my breath was pulled from my lungs. Waves of pleasure coursed through me, and I squeezed his ass with my legs, afraid he'd leave my core before I was done.

Just as quickly as I had tensed up, every muscle loosened until I was a pile of bliss.

I blinked my eyes open just as Trevor let go of one of my hands and wrapped his fingers lightly around my neck.

"I've been waiting to kiss you again since you dropped me off at the airport." Not letting go, he took my mouth as he began to thrust into me.

He felt amazing as he moved in and out of me, and his kisses were like fire. I ran my hand down his back. I wanted to touch him everywhere just to make sure what was happening was real.

As his pace quickened and his strokes got harder, he released my lips and stared into my soul. Just as his climax hit, my eyes widened as I felt his seed inside me, and I surprisingly came again.

Trevor's upper body collapsed on top of me as the hand around my neck loosened and fell away. He managed to find enough energy to roll to his side, taking me with him.

"Holy shit," he muttered, wrapping his arm around my waist and pulling my lower body snug with his. He was still inside me, and this pushed me deeper. "I don't want to ever leave."

I smiled and kissed his chest. "I'd like to think I'm that good, but it's probably the no-condom thing."

He shook his head, his chin rubbing the top of my

head. "No. Lorraine and I dated for a long time, so we didn't use anything but the pill. It's all you, Alexis."

My smile turned into a grin. "Be careful, or I'll get a big head."

"As long as I get to fuck you again, I don't care."

I planted soft kisses on his neck and hoped he liked the next thing I said. "We are married. Don't you think we should be able to enjoy each other while we stay that way? It's only fair. We're not sleeping with anyone else."

He rolled us, so I was on my back again. "That's good because now that I've been inside you"—he cupped my breast and sucked on the tip—"you're mine."

I hadn't known Trevor would be this possessive. Our marriage was only temporary, but I couldn't stop the thought that I wanted to be his forever.

Chapter Twenty-Three

TREVOR

THE NEXT MORNING, I kissed Alexis's naked back and slipped out of bed. I didn't wake her, figuring she needed her sleep.

After I'd caught her with her vibrator and we had amazing sex, we'd gone back outside before everyone began to wonder about us. But as soon as we'd finished dinner, we'd gone back to bed, so we could screw again.

I hated to think of my brother when I thought of my wife, but the guy was absolutely nuts to let someone like Alexis go. She was kind, successful, and determined. She loved her family, and she was phenomenal in bed. I didn't think a man could ask for a better partner.

And speaking of my brother, Kevin was sitting at the dining room table when I walked out of my bedroom. He was staring at his phone and didn't bother looking up as I got closer.

There was a large bowl of fruit on the table, and I popped a strawberry in my mouth.

"Good morning," I said, full of cheer. I couldn't be anything but happy after last night.

Kevin pursed his lips and looked up at me. "Did you have a good night?" he said with a sneer.

"Yeah, it was great. Why do you ask?"

His nostrils flared. "We share a wall."

"Oops," I said, not the least bit remorseful. I pulled out a chair, grabbed a clean plate from the tabletop, and loaded it with more fruit.

"Weird that I didn't hear you two the night before."

Weird that I haven't heard you and Candace either night.

"I don't know what you're trying to insinuate," I said, not looking at my brother. "But Alexis fell asleep, crying in my arms because you'd let Nana think that Alexis never wanted children. Then, you knocked up someone that Alexis had let live in her home and cared about." I met his eyes. "And I don't fuck my wife when she's sad and upset."

Kevin had the decency to look sheepish. "I didn't tell Nana that. She just assumed."

I stabbed a piece of cantaloupe with my fork. "Because you let her think that."

He clenched his jaw. "I'll talk to her and tell her the truth."

"I already did it for you."

The click of my bedroom door opening sounded behind me, and Kevin and I both turned to see Alexis walk out in one of my T-shirts.

"Good morning," she said when she reached the table.

I hauled her onto my lap and kissed her. "Good morning, Lexie." After last night, I wasn't going to try to keep my hands off her anymore.

She smiled at my use of the nickname. "Can I have some of your fruit?" she asked.

I gave her my fork. "Eat away."

As she took a bite, I put my hand on her thigh and ran it up and under the hem of my shirt. "Ooh," I whispered. I hadn't expected her to be completely naked underneath.

She grinned at me. "I was too hungry to waste time with underwear."

Kevin cleared his throat, and the two of us looked in his direction.

"Could you not?" he asked.

Alexis pointed the fork at him. "If I have to watch you with Candace, you can watch me with Trevor."

I snickered.

The front door opened, and Candace and Nana walked in. Everyone's attention turned to them.

"You're awake," Nana said, looking at me and Alexis, who stiffened in my arms.

Alexis tried to get up, but I pulled her back down.

"Your grandmother," she said to me in a tight voice.

"Relax. You're my wife." I raised my voice to Nana and Candace. "Where did you go?"

"We went to the park where the wedding is taking place on Saturday," Candace said.

"It was beautiful," Nana informed us. "It's a great place for memories. Don't you think, Candace?"

Candace was looking down at her phone.

"Candace?" Nana said.

Candace looked up. "What? Oh. Yes, it's beautiful." She forced a smile.

"Is everything all right?" Alexis asked.

Candace was clearly not as happy as she was trying to show us she was. And I couldn't help but notice that Alexis had observed enough about her mood to ask, but her own fiancé hadn't.

"Yes. Everything is fine." Candace didn't want to talk about it.

"What's on the agenda today? Do you have to do other wedding stuff?" I asked.

"No," Candace said. "Kevin took care of everything before we came down here. And really, we only have the officiant and a photographer for half an hour."

"No flowers?" Alexis asked. "We should at least get you a bouquet and something for your mom."

"My parents aren't coming."

Nana gasped.

"*What?*" Alexis asked, visibly shocked.

"It's only going to be the five of us at the wedding," Kevin explained.

"Your parents aren't coming?" Alexis repeated. "I assumed they were meeting us here in a couple days."

Candace hugged her stomach. "They weren't very happy about the baby. We aren't speaking much."

"I'm so sorry," Alexis said.

"It's fine," Candace quickly answered back. "I'm going to go lie down for a bit."

After she left the room, we all looked at Kevin.

"What's going on?" I asked.

"Nothing. Her parents aren't happy she's pregnant, which is why we're getting married so fast. They didn't want to try to get passports at the last minute."

Alexis slowly shook her head. "That's so sad."

"Doesn't she have a friend or two who would come to be with her?" I asked.

"None of her friends from Canada could come for the same reason, and her few friends in Minnesota couldn't afford it."

"And you didn't offer to pay for at least one of them?"

Kevin frowned. "No."

"Unbelievable," Alexis muttered. She jumped off my lap and headed to our bedroom.

"I'm with her," I said. "You paid for all of us to come here. You could have offered for one more person to come."

"It's not that easy," Kevin said.

I stood and shook my head in disappointment. "I'm going to go get dressed."

Alexis was on her phone, sitting on the bed, when I walked into our room.

"Can you believe him?" she asked me, looking up.

"No. But also yes."

"He's the worst." She turned her eyes back to her screen.

"What are you doing?"

"Trying to find one of Candace's friends on social media. She had a few come over when she lived with us. I'm hoping I can find someone, so Candace isn't so alone."

I sat next to her. "I thought you were mad at her?"

"I'm mad, but I don't hate her. No one deserves to be alone on their wedding day."

I grinned at her.

Alexis glanced at me. "What?" she said when she saw my expression.

"Nothing."

"Then, why are you smiling like that?"

"You're just an amazing person, is all." One I could see myself falling in love with.

Chapter Twenty-Four

TREVOR

"OH MY GOD, Candace's friend said she can come," Alexis said way too early the next morning.

I grunted in response, keeping my eyes shut. I was not ready to wake up yet.

"Okay, so I have to get Summer a plane ticket and a hotel room. And then do I tell Candace her friend is coming, or do I make it a surprise?"

I made another noise.

"I'm going to make it a surprise. This is going to be so awesome."

At this point, I was sure she was talking to herself and didn't require me to stay awake.

"*Trevor.*"

"What?" I whined. "I'm sleeping. Can't we talk about this later? Please?"

"I'm way too excited to sleep."

"Okay. Wake me in an hour then."

"Or..."

She started shifting around in the bed, and I almost opened my eyes to see what she was doing, but then I knew I'd be up for the day.

I told myself I didn't care what she was doing.

Until she put my dick in her mouth.

My eyes flew open, and I pushed the covers off me.

She pulled my shaft out of her mouth and smiled. "What? I thought you were too tired to get up?" She ran her tongue around the head.

"You are evil. I have half a mind to push you off and go back to sleep."

She laughed. "You would never."

I sighed. "You're right. I would never." I patted my mouth. "Now, turn around so that I can eat that beautiful pussy."

"In a minute. Let me enjoy this first."

I grinned and put my hands behind my head. "What the lady wants, the lady gets."

Alexis took me in her mouth again as the doorbell rang in the main room. I didn't pay much mind to it until I heard my brother shout Alexis's name, and pounding footsteps got closer to our bedroom door.

Right before the door swung open, I pushed her behind me as I sat up to block her.

"Get the fuck out of our room," I commanded.

Kevin didn't even look at me as he waved a manila envelope and a stack of papers in his hand. "You changed your last name?" he said to Alexis, who was peeking around my shoulder. "For him?" He pointed his finger at me. "But you wouldn't for me?"

Kevin must have gotten a report from Kelly Investigations. That had to be what he was holding.

"If I didn't know better, I would think you're jealous, brother." I tilted my head. "Also, how do you know this?"

"I'm not jealous, and I have my ways," he said, sticking his chin in the air.

"You mean, like hiring someone to investigate us?" I said.

Kevin sputtered, trying to come up with a response. "It doesn't matter," he finally shouted. "That's not why I came in here. I want to know why she changed her last name for you and not me."

For a second, I thought my brother looked hurt, but then he sneered.

"I should have known you would though. It's always been Trevor, never me."

I quickly looked at Alexis. *What did my brother mean by that?*

But she was looking at Kevin. "Get over yourself. At the end of the day, it's my name, and what I choose to do with it is my business."

"I can't believe you would do this."

"And I can't believe you claimed to love me but had no problem leaving me without even giving me the share of the money allocated to me."

He had the audacity to look offended. "You're bringing that up now? I thought you were over it."

"You owe me half of a five- to six-hundred-thousand-dollar house that had no mortgage. And it's not about being greedy. Do you know where I've been living this whole time? No. Because you're a selfish asshole. And I was never over it. I just stopped asking you about it." She put her hand on my arm. "And I changed my last name because I felt like it was the right thing to do with Trevor."

Kevin's eyes shot to me. "Don't be fooled. She only changed her last name because she wants part of Nelson Pharmacy. What better way than to have the last name of the store? And she only did it to get back at me. Watch out for her, Trevor."

The joke was on my brother. I already knew Alexis's full intentions.

"If I did it to get back at you, then why didn't I tell you right away?" Alexis pointed out.

Kevin didn't have a response.

"Also, asshole, Trevor and I have a prenup. His inheritance is all his."

"I don't believe you."

"Don't then." Alexis shrugged. "I don't really give a shit either way. The only reason I'm here, acting like we're a happy family, is because of your grandmother. That poor woman doesn't need to know what a dick her grandson is."

"Yeah, well, she doesn't need to know that her other grandson has a slut for a wife who will spread her legs for any—"

Kevin didn't get to finish his sentence because I flew off the bed and slammed him against the wall by his throat. "Don't you ever, *ever* speak to my wife or any woman like that ever again." I pushed him out the door. "Get out of here, you piece of shit."

I slammed the door closed and fell against it.

Alexis ran her hand through her hair. "This morning started out so well." She sighed. "Good mood ruined."

I walked back over to the bed and collapsed on it. "Well, that was a real shitshow."

Alexis lay back. "I wonder how much your grandma heard."

I groaned. I hadn't even thought of that. "I'll talk to her in a bit and try to smooth things over. But I swear, if she wasn't here, I would put us on the next plane home."

She kissed my cheek. "I appreciate that, but let's not let him ruin the time we have left here. It's still a nice vacation spot. The wedding is tomorrow, and we can leave after that. We don't have to stay the whole weekend."

"Are you still going to have Candace's friend come?"

"Yes. I feel bad she's marrying Kevin. Baby or no baby, she's better off without him. Maybe her friend can talk her out of getting married to him."

Chapter Twenty-Five

ALEXIS

KEVIN LEFT the house after the fight on Friday without a word of where he was going. Thankfully, he left the car, so Trevor, Adele, and I went to a flower shop to get some flowers for Candace. When we told the florist it was for Candace's wedding, she insisted on making a bouquet. It wasn't extravagant because it was last minute, but it was beautiful. We also picked out a boutonniere for Adele and one for the groom. If he ever came back.

Which he did, late that night.

And the next morning, he acted like nothing had happened the day before. But at least Candace wasn't getting stood up at the altar.

"Oh no," I said, looking at my phone. I'd been admiring Trevor in his towel after he showered when I heard my phone alert for a text message.

Trevor dried his chest off. "What's wrong?"

"Summer's layover was delayed. She might be late for the wedding. There is no way I can go pick her up now."

He pulled a shirt on. "Tell her we'll pay for her ride and give her the address for where the wedding is located."

I sent a quick text to Summer.

"Fingers crossed she makes it just in time."

"I'm sure Candace will be happy to see Summer even if the ceremony is over."

I fell back on the bed. "It would be nice if something went right today."

Trevor dropped down next to me and propped his head up with his hand. "You have me." He grinned.

"You're right. I do." I brushed my hand over his cheek. "Is this thing we're doing here—the sex—something we're going to keep doing once we go back home?"

He frowned. "Why wouldn't we?"

"I don't know. Because sex was never part of this arrangement. I didn't know if it was a vacation thing."

His eyebrows lifted. "Do you want to stop?"

I really wanted him to answer before me because if our answers didn't match, I was going to feel like a fool.

"No."

"I don't either."

I smiled.

"I mean, how am I supposed to go back to not having sex when I have you ready and waiting for me every day?" he joked.

I pushed him back as I stood. "When you put it like that, I'll go back to my vibrator."

Snagging me around the waist, he yanked me back down. "Now that you have me, you don't need that vibrator. Unless I'm in the room too."

"Are you telling me what to do?"

"Yes."

I laughed because I'd thought he would deny that he was bossing me around.

"Tell you what. I'll save my vibrator for when you're sick or out of town." I didn't know why I'd said that. We probably weren't going to be together that long.

"Hmm...deal. But only if you're thinking about me the whole time."

"You and my latest celebrity crush," I countered.

"Fine."

I laughed again, as if he had any control of my fantasies.

"And what about you?" I asked.

He frowned. "What about me?"

"What do you use when you're alone?"

"My fist."

I supposed that made sense. Men used fewer sex toys than women.

"And who do you think about?" I had never heard him talk about actresses or models before. I really didn't know who he would like.

"Lately? You, so we're good there."

My mouth dropped open just as Nana called Trevor's name.

"I'd better go check on her," he said and scooted off the mattress.

"Trevor?" I said right before he walked out the door.

"Yeah?"

"Were you just joking?"

"About what?" His brow furrowed. "About telling you when you can and can't use your vibrator? I thought you knew I was."

"No, not that. Were you joking about thinking about me when you masturbate?"

He grinned. "Nope. Not since you said yes." He turned and walked out the door. "What do you need, Nana?"

I grabbed my phone and brought up my text message thread with my friends. I'd been so busy that I hadn't told them anything about what was going on.

> Me: So…Trevor and I had sex.

> Tessa: I knew it!

> Me: What?

> Tessa: Never mind. When did it happen? How? I want all the deets.

Paisley: Yeah, baby!

Bree: Get it!

Me: It happened a few days ago. I had to put sunscreen on him and almost embarrassed myself in front of the rest of the family. He must have sensed my sexual frustration because he followed me into the house.

Isabelle: Woohoo! I'm so glad you did the deed. And I bet it didn't complicate anything either.

I rolled my eyes at her reference to our dinner conversation.

Me: Nobody likes a know-it-all.

Isabelle: Ha. I was right.

Pru: I just want to know if it was good. You all are getting some; meanwhile, my pussy is about to pack up and find someplace else to live.

Me: Welcome to the convo, Pru. And that shit is funny, but I'm sure your pussy is perfectly happy without a man. And yes, the sex was good. Better than. It was phenomenal.

Bree: And way better than his brother?

Me: Bree, now, I would never compare brothers like that.

Tessa: If you don't tell us, we're going to assume that Kevin is better.

Me: Take that back. Trevor is clearly the winner. He knows exactly how to use his body, and he knows what a female orgasm is. Kevin, not so much.

Isabelle: Burn.

Me: He deserves it.

I told them all about how he'd burst into my and Trevor's bedroom, acting like an asshole.

Bree: Yep, he deserves it. I feel bad for his wife.

Me: Future wife. We have a couple more hours until they're married. Maybe she'll change her mind.

Isabelle: Do you want her to? They kind of deserve each other.

Bree: She's young. Her brain isn't fully developed. I feel bad for her actually.

Pru: You're too nice.

Me: Well, we're not going to be best friends or anything, but I have some sympathy for her. With the baby, she's now tied to Kevin for the rest of her life even if she wants a divorce.

Tessa: I think it shows what a caring person you are.

Me: Thanks.

Me: Where's Elizabeth?

Isabelle: She's doing something with her family. She didn't say what it was, just that it was important. I'm sure she'll catch up later.

Me: Well, I'd better go. I have a wedding to stop. I mean, get ready for.

Me: Just kidding.

I got some LOLs and laughing emojis.

Me: Later, ladies. See you when I get back!

Chapter Twenty-Six

TREVOR

I TOOK Alexis's hand in mine. "She'll be here."

She turned and looked over her shoulder for what felt like the fifth time. "I keep telling myself that, but what if she gets stuck in traffic or something?"

I kissed her hand. "Her plane already landed. She's in a Lyft. She'll get here soon."

We were sitting in the park where the wedding was being held, just waiting for the ceremony to start.

Even though the area was small with only a few rows of chairs, it looked sad because it was so empty. Nana was sitting on the groom's side, and Alexis and I sat on the bride's side. I'd told Nana it only seemed fair for us to split up. Especially since I knew Alexis would rather not sit on Kevin's side of the aisle.

"I was just so hoping Summer would get here before the wedding started."

"Do you want me to go and stall it?"

Her face lit up. "You'd do that?"

"Babe, I was joking." I felt bad she'd thought I was serious.

"Right."

"But look, the officiant isn't even at the front yet."

No sooner had the words come out of my mouth than a man walked up, who was clearly there to marry the bride and groom. He took his position in the small gazebo.

Alexis looked at me.

"Whoops." I squeezed her hand. "It'll be okay."

Kevin walked up sixty seconds later.

"She's only two minutes away," Alexis whispered, clearly relieved. She put her head on my shoulder as Kevin hit play on his phone, which was connected to the portable speaker sitting behind the officiant.

I put my arm around her. I loved that she wasn't afraid to be close to me anymore. I should have taken her to bed right away. I could get used to this feeling that our marriage was real.

"Please rise," the officiant said.

We stood and turned to watch Candace walk down the short aisle.

As we turned to face the front again, Alexis, who still had her phone in her hand, looked down and frowned.

"What's wrong?"

She showed me her screen.

Summer: I'm here.

Summer: And I'm sorry.

"What the hell does that mean?" I asked.

"I have no idea."

Candace gasped at something behind us, but her reaction wasn't happiness. It was panic. We all spun to see what she was looking at.

A woman around Candace's age, who I assumed was her friend Summer, was heading toward us. But behind her was a young man who looked to be about the same age.

"Did Summer bring a boyfriend? I thought she was coming alone."

"That's not Summer's boyfriend. That's Xavier. Candace used to date him." Suddenly, she clutched my arm. "Oh no. I bet Summer is dating Candace's old boyfriend, and she brought him to the wedding. That must be why she sent me the sorry text. I know Candace is getting married, but it will still hurt."

"Ouch. Karma sure is a bitch," I muttered. "Candace dates your ex-husband, and her friend dates her ex-boyfriend."

"This is all my fault."

I pulled her close. "You couldn't have known about any of this."

Summer ran up to the row behind us and straight to

Alexis. "I'm so sorry. When he found out I was coming, he insisted on coming with."

"Why? Just to show that he's with you now?"

Summer recoiled. "I'm not *with* him."

"Then, what is he doing here?" Alexis asked.

"What are you doing here?" Candace asked him, and everyone pivoted around to see what was going to happen next.

"Shut off the music," Xavier said. He was a tall, lanky kid with messy blond hair, wearing worn jeans and a white T-shirt. He didn't look like a wedding guest.

The music was cut.

"Can you get to the part where you ask if anyone objects to this marriage or whatever it is you say?" Xavier asked the officiant.

"I haven't even started," the older man said, eyes wide.

"Okay, right. Well, I object to this wedding."

Candace left Kevin's side. "You can't do that," she hissed as she marched toward him. "I gave you a chance."

"I fucked up, okay? But you can't marry *that* guy," Xavier said, pointing to Kevin.

I really didn't know what to do in this situation, but Candace was going to be my sister-in-law soon, and she obviously didn't want Xavier there.

"Candace, would you like me to escort this guy to his car?" I asked.

"*No,*" they both answered me.

"He can leave on his own," Candace said.

"I flew all the way down here for you."

She lifted her chin. "It's too late."

"Tell me you love that guy, and I'll leave."

"Please, just go," Candace pleaded.

"You can't say it because you don't."

I felt for Xavier, but Candace was having my brother's baby, and I didn't blame her for wanting to get married to the father of her child.

I put my hand on Xavier's shoulder. "Look, I'm sorry you came all this way, but she has clearly chosen who she wants to be with. Think about the baby."

Xavier knocked my hand off. "I am thinking about the baby. I'm the father. That's my baby."

Chapter Twenty-Seven

ALEXIS

"*WHAT?*" The word came flying out of my mouth and pretty much everyone else's, except Candace, Xavier, and Summer. And Kevin.

"You knew," Trevor said, looking right at his brother.

Kevin stood, unmoving, but then slowly nodded his head.

I sat down, glancing up at Summer over my shoulder. "So, this is why you were sorry." It came out more like a statement than a question.

"Yes. When you asked me to come to the wedding, I told a friend who told a friend who told Xavier."

"That's something you should have done," Xavier said.

Summer frowned at him. "You told Candace you didn't want anything to do with her when she told you that she was pregnant."

Xavier's head swung around to Candace. "That's what you told people?"

Candace wrung her hands against her chest. "Uh..."

Xavier looked at Trevor. "She told me the night before I had to leave for a yearly family vacation. And when I got back home, she had left for Canada with no way to contact her. She blocked me on all social media. I've been trying to find her for months, only to discover she's back in Minnesota and getting married to someone else."

I stood and put my hands up. "I think we all need to take a deep breath."

Adele looked like she was going to pass out.

"Trevor, I think you need to check on your grandmother. Candace, I think you and Xavier need to talk. Kevin, I think you can come down from there because it doesn't seem like you're getting married right now."

Trevor, noticing the same thing I had, rushed over to his grandma with Kevin following.

Candace didn't move.

"You might as well have a conversation and get it over with," I told her. "Ignoring your problem won't make it go away."

"All right," she agreed. "Let's go over there," she told Xavier.

As soon as they were gone, I went to check on Adele. "Is everything okay?"

"I'm fine," Adele said right away.

"Nana, you don't look fine," Trevor said.

"I meant, I'm fine physically."

"Are you sure it's not your heart?" Kevin asked.

"I have cancer, not a heart condition," she snapped back at him. "And it seems I have a grandson who lied to me."

Kevin looked at his feet. "I'm sorry, Nana. I didn't mean for you to get caught up in this mess."

"So, you knew the baby wasn't yours?" Trevor asked.

"Yes. Candace and I aren't even in a relationship. I was helping her out. When her parents found out she was pregnant, they wanted nothing to do with her. She told me the father of the baby had left her as well. I didn't know it was Xavier or that she had lied about the circumstances."

"You didn't need to marry her," I pointed out.

He turned his eyes away from us. "When I found out that Nana had cancer, I figured Candace and I could help each other out."

Trevor frowned. "But you told me you were getting married the same day Nana told us."

"I might have already known."

Trevor's jaw tensed. "Might have or already did?" he asked through clenched teeth.

"I already did, okay?"

"How long?" Trevor demanded.

"How long what?" Kevin looked genuinely confused even though I thought the question was obvious.

"How long did you know?"

"A month?" Kevin shrugged.

"And you didn't tell me?"

"Oh, so you could go and marry my ex-wife even sooner?"

Trevor's eyes narrowed to the point that I couldn't even see what color they were. "No, you fucking asshole. You could have told me so that I could spend more time with our grandmother before she passes away."

"How did you even know?" I couldn't help but ask.

"She had already gone to her regular doctor. I was there when he called her, and I overheard part of her conversation. I didn't actually know, *know* until she went to the specialist and told us at dinner."

"Don't try digging yourself out of this hole now," Trevor said. "You heard enough to find a wife, so you must have felt pretty strongly about what was said when her doctor called."

"Please stop fighting, boys," Adele said, but I didn't think Kevin and Trevor heard her.

"I did what I had to do—" Kevin started until I cut him off.

"*Stop*," I commanded.

Both men shut their mouths and looked at me.

"Please stop fighting," Adele begged.

"You're right," Trevor said. "I'm sorry, Nana."

"I'm sorry too," Kevin said.

"Can we just go home?" Adele asked.

"I'll get the car and take you back to the rental," Trevor said.

"No. I want to go home to Minnesota."

Trevor met my eyes. It was early afternoon, but I didn't know if there would be any flights available.

"I'll see what I can do," I told Adele, digging my phone out of my pocket. "It might be late when we get back, and it might cost extra." I pulled up our airline customer service number, figuring it would be the fastest way to get our flights switched.

"I don't care. I just want to be done with Florida."

"Let's get you back to the house to pack then," Trevor said.

He helped his grandmother stand, and she looked at Kevin.

"I can't believe you were going to marry that girl for your inheritance." She swung her head to Trevor. "Next, you're going to tell me your marriage is fake too."

I quickly looked at my phone, ready to call the airport.

Candace and Xavier came back at that time.

Candace took a deep breath. "I'm sorry, Kevin, but I can't marry you."

"I figured."

"Kevin told us about your parents," I said. "What are you going to do?"

"I'm not sure what the long-term plans are, but I'm

moving in with Xavier and his parents." She smiled at the young man. "They're going to help with the baby while he goes to school. And maybe I can get an education visa and go to college too."

I hadn't even thought about all the technical aspects of having Candace stay in America. "Did you come on a marriage visa or whatever they're called?"

Her smile fell as she looked worried. "Yes, and they might not accept changing my visa."

"Don't worry. I will have the immigration lawyer look into it," Kevin said. "I promised I would get you to the US, and I plan to keep that promise."

I stared at him in wonder, and I realized that once upon a time, I had married him for a reason. It was nice to see that he was doing something good, and I was relieved to know he hadn't messed around with our exchange student or cheated on me.

He wasn't completely innocent in this situation, but he wasn't the terrible man I had previously thought.

Chapter Twenty-Eight

ALEXIS

"HEY, ALEXIS, WE'RE HOME."

I blinked the sleep from my eyes and sat up as I rubbed my neck. We'd gotten back to Minnesota around nine at night. We'd had to drive Adele an hour home, unload her bags from the car, and drive all the way back to the Twin Cities. I must have dozed off somewhere along the way.

As we carried our stuff inside, I said, "That was a family vacation I will never forget."

Trevor laughed. "Me neither."

I picked up my suitcase, lugged it upstairs, and put it on the bed in my room. I unzipped the top, opened it, and stared at the mess that awaited me. *Forget this.*

"I'm unpacking tomorrow," I called out to Trevor. "I'm way too tired to do this right now."

"I hope that's the only thing you're too tired for," he

said from behind me as he slipped his arms around my waist, pulling me close.

I rested my head on his shoulder. "Hmm. Well, I did take a nap, so I could probably muster up a little energy for something. What do you have in mind?"

In an instant, he swung me up into his arms and carried me to his bedroom.

As soon as he set me on the bed, he took his shirt and socks off. I stripped off my clothes and went to help him with the rest of his.

"Whoa. I thought you were tired," he said.

"Seeing you almost naked refreshed me." I quickly pushed his pants off his hips. I sighed. "It's so perfect."

I yanked Trevor onto the bed and sucked his cock into my mouth. His scent was strong, and the flavor of his skin hit my tongue immediately. Normally, I was all for showering after being on an airplane, but I loved smelling him rather than soap.

I bobbed my head on his cock and massaged his balls, trying to memorize the feel of them. Trevor cupped the back of my neck, his hand tightening every time I went down.

Soon, his fingers were squeezing more than they were loosening, and I knew he had to be getting close. I had yet to taste him since we'd been interrupted the other day when I was giving him head, and I couldn't wait to find out what it was like when he came in my mouth.

The thought of it turned me on so much that I could feel my wetness between my thighs. *I wonder if I can come from giving head.* It had never happened before, but there was a first time for everything.

Trevor fisted my hair as he cried out and spilled onto my tongue. He was hot and salty, and I made sure to swallow every last drop.

I dragged him from my mouth when his orgasm was finished and couldn't resist licking his length one more time.

His cock jerked as he grunted, and I smiled at my accomplishment.

Trevor lifted me under my arms and threw me down on the bed. I hadn't been ready, and I screamed and laughed in surprise.

"What are you doing?" I asked.

He ran his tongue over his bottom lip. "It's your turn."

Suddenly, I remembered the whole plane ride and not-bathing situation.

I closed my legs. Or tried to. His head stopped me.

"I should probably shower first. We were traveling a long time today."

"Shut up."

My jaw dropped open. "What?"

"You heard me. Shut up. If I want to eat your pussy, I'm going to eat your pussy. I don't care if you've been traveling for ten days. Now, open those pretty thighs for me."

As I did, I said, "I can't believe you told me to shut up."

Trevor put his entire mouth on my pussy and sucked. "I had to get your attention somehow." He drew my lips apart and brushed his teeth against my taut clit.

My hips twitched. "Oh, you have it," I said on a long sigh.

Trevor used both hands to lift my ass and gave me the best head of my life. I had never known what other women meant when they said men feasted on them, but I did now. He licked and sucked every inch of me as if he couldn't get enough.

When I neared my climax, he sensed it and turned all his attention to my very swollen nub. A few hard flicks of his tongue, and I was soaring as waves of pleasure crashed over me.

He gently set my butt back on the bed and crawled up next to me. We faced each other as he pulled my leg over his hips. With one smooth thrust, he was inside me, and I nipped his neck as he filled me.

Trevor ran his hands down my back and pulled me closer. "Now that we both already came, I can make love to you nice and slow."

Chapter Twenty-Nine

ALEXIS

THE NEXT MORNING WAS SUNDAY, and since we'd come home a day early, I didn't have to hurry to get up for work. Although I had already texted Tessa that I would be in later that day. I'd also promised to tell her everything when I arrived at the café.

Right now, I was enjoying lying next to my sleeping husband and simply watching him.

His eyes were closed, so I was surprised when he said, "Are you staring at me?"

He'd caught me.

"Maybe. A little."

"What are you thinking about?"

I laughed.

"What's so funny?"

"I'm a woman. I'm thinking about a lot of things. Would you like me to list them all?"

"Sure."

I'd thought he'd say no, but he'd surprised me again.

"I'm thinking I need to go into work, how Tessa might have had too much to do without me, if you and I need to stay married now that Kevin didn't marry Candace, about how your grandma is feeling this morning, when I should have my attorney send Kevin's lawyer the paperwork because a part of me feels bad for him, that I have to unpack and do laundry, and how I haven't called my mom yet to do a mother-daughter date. I'm also thinking that I want to pull the covers over my head and not worry about anything." I took a deep breath. "I think that's it."

Trevor blinked at me. "That's...a lot."

"I know."

He brushed the hair off my cheek. "I can help with a couple of things."

I lifted my brow. "Really?"

He chuckled. "Really. I'll call Nana this morning to see how she's doing. Absolutely send those papers to my brother. Did he feel bad for you? No."

"Got it."

"Take the morning to do things around the house, like unpack and call your mom. Go into work this afternoon. I will do laundry today."

I smiled. "I can work with that."

"I figured you would. And, yes, we need to stay married. You still need your money, and I still need my inheritance. Even with Kevin not getting married, I don't meet my grandfather's requirements without you."

Despite us still needing each other for these two things, I liked that I'd get to be with him a little longer. I wasn't ready for our time to end.

"And as for the last thing..." He hauled me into his arms. "I can't make all your worries go away, but I can pull the covers over us and make you forget about them for a while."

I wiggled my eyebrows. "I like the sound of that."

———

TREVOR

I watched my beautiful, naked wife crawl out of bed and stretch, in awe of the female form.

"I need to shower," she said.

"You can use the one in here." As far as I was concerned, this was her bedroom and bathroom now.

"All my stuff is in the main one."

"Move it in here."

"I don't know. I kind of like not sharing."

I smiled. "I don't blame you." I threw myself to the other side of the bed and lightly smacked her ass. "You go shower. I'll call my grandma."

Alexis left, and I rang Nana.

"Hello?"

"Morning, Nana. How are you?"

"Glad to be home."

"Same here. Are you feeling all right?"

She made an exasperated sound. "I'm fine, Trevor."

"Okay, okay. I was just checking. Alexis was worried about you."

"Alexis, hmm?"

I grinned. "And me too. Yesterday was stressful."

"It was, but you don't have to worry about me."

"When is your next doctor appointment?"

"I'm not sure. I'll let you know and call you back."

I frowned, not quite believing her. "Are you really going to call me back?"

"Yes. Who is the grandmother here, and who is the grandson?"

"I'm simply worried, is all. I would like to go with you to your next appointment, if that's okay."

"I'll call you back, Trevor."

"I love you," I quickly added before she could hang up on me.

"I love you too."

I ended my call and made a mental note to call her back in a day or two if she didn't ring me.

As I set my phone down, I got a text message notification.

"No way." My grandmother didn't know how to text.

And I was right. It was my brother.

> Kevin: Tell your wife I called a realtor today. She can lay off me.

I didn't know what he was referring to.

> Me: I'll tell her the first part, but I don't know what you're talking about with the second part.

> Kevin: She hired a lawyer. My lawyer left me a message while I was out of town, and I just got it. Tell her thanks for kicking me while I'm down.

I rolled my eyes.

> Me: You're fine. You have plenty of money. You don't even have to sell your house. Just pay her half of what it's worth.

The three bubbles appeared and then went away. Appeared and went away.

When he finally responded, I was surprised.

> Kevin: I'm still going to sell. Now that I'm alone, there's no point in keeping it. I wanted a nice place for the baby, but I don't need it anymore.

I thought my brother was actually sad that he was out of Candace and her baby's lives.

> **Me:** I'm sure you will find someone else. You're still young. And for what it's worth, I appreciate you doing the right thing.

> **Kevin:** Yeah, thanks. I'll let you know when the sale is final. And I'll have my lawyer get the money to Alexis.

> **Me:** Thank you.

"Why do you look like you saw a miracle or something?"

I lifted my head to see Alexis standing in the doorway. She was dressed, but her hair was in a towel.

"Nana is doing well, and the reason I have this particular expression on my face is because Kevin just texted me to tell me he's selling his house."

Her jaw dropped, and she started laughing. "What? How?"

"Your lawyer didn't listen to you. He sent over the paperwork to Kevin's lawyer while we were out of town. Kevin just found out, and he wanted me to let you know you can leave him alone now."

"Gladly." Alexis ran toward me and landed in my arms. "This is the best news. Everything is coming together now."

Chapter Thirty

ALEXIS

THREE WEEKS LATER, I got my money from Kevin. He hadn't closed on our old house yet, but he had a buyer, and it was in escrow.

The day I got my check, I walked into work, and Tessa and the rest of our friends were waiting. They all started clapping the second I entered.

Bursting into laughter, I waved at them to stop. "You ladies are silly. You're applauding me like I made some great accomplishment."

Tessa brought over a glass of champagne. "It's sparkling apple cider since it's the middle of the workday. And this *is* a great accomplishment," she pointed out.

"I know, but it's not like I did the work. It was Trevor and his lawyer."

"We're still happy for you," Bree said.

"Thanks. I'm happy for me too," I joked.

"So, what are you going to do with your money?" Paisley asked.

I chuckled. "It's not a million dollars or anything, but I'm definitely going to get a house. Nothing huge, but someplace that is my own."

"What about Trevor?" Elizabeth asked.

"What do you mean?"

"I thought maybe you two would stay together."

The thought had crossed my mind more than once or twice. I was really happy, being with him. He loved it when I brought home cupcakes, and he made love to me every night. But he never talked about us staying together, so I didn't either.

I didn't want my friends to know that it made me sad to think about not being with him, so I smiled. "Nah. He has his life, and I have mine. We're friends."

"Friends who are having sex," Pru teased.

"Hey. If we're going to be stuck together, we might as well enjoy each other, right?"

"I agree," Bree said.

"Besides, Adele is still doing well. We just saw her yesterday. She came to our house, and she was dressed up and had her makeup on. She's really holding on."

My phone rang, and I saw it was Trevor.

"Ooh...speak of the devil..."

"It's Trevor's grandma?" Isabelle asked.

"No, silly," Elizabeth said. "It's Trevor."

Isabelle hit her palm on her head, so I was laughing when I answered the phone. "Hello?"

"Alexis?"

Ice immediately went through my veins. His tone was too serious.

"What's wrong?"

"Nana's gone."

I closed my eyes as tears filled them. "I'm so sorry, Trevor."

"Can you come home?"

"Yes. I'll be right there."

I hung up the phone as six pairs of eyes stared at me in sympathy.

"That was—"

"We know, honey," Tessa said. "Go home."

————

Adele's funeral was packed with people from her small town. Trevor held my hand throughout the whole thing, unwilling to let go. I knew it was for his benefit more than mine.

Even knowing that she was going to pass and that she was no longer in pain now—pain that she had hidden from us—he was still sad and grieving.

But I thought it brought him some comfort to see all the people who had come to honor her presence.

Kevin was also there, alone, and for what it was worth, he also seemed sad.

After the service, a man who was probably in his late fifties with salt-and-pepper hair approached the two brothers. Trevor immediately shook his hand.

"I'm sorry for your loss," the man said.

"Thank you," Trevor said while Kevin nodded.

"Vernon, this is my wife, Alexis," Trevor said, introducing me. "Alexis, this is Vernon. He runs Nelson Pharmacy."

Vernon smiled at me. "I'm the general manager. I can't take all the credit. I have good employees."

"Don't be so modest," Trevor said. "You've worked at Nelson Pharmacy since college. You do a lot for the store."

"He has?" Kevin asked.

Vernon smiled. "I have, and thank you, but I only came over to express my condolences."

"Thank you," Trevor said.

Vernon gave us a wave and walked away.

"He is probably worried about his job now that Nana is dead."

Trevor and I both looked at Kevin. Just when I thought he wasn't that bad of a guy, he said something like that.

"Of course he is," Trevor said. "He's worked there since college. It's all he knows. And he has five kids, two of whom still live at home." He shook his head. "Come on, Alexis. I can't with him today."

After the funeral, we had a reception at his grandmother's house. Trevor was very polite to everyone, but after a few hours, I could tell the socializing was wearing on him. Thankfully, people began to notice and started taking their leave. We were left with one man, dressed in a suit that looked too fancy for a funeral.

Trevor and Kevin had gone into the kitchen to clean up the food, so I approached him.

"Is there anything I can help you with?" I asked him, hoping he'd get the hint and leave.

"Yes, I'm Mr. Randolph. I'm here to speak with Trevor and Kevin Nelson."

"I'm sorry, but the reception is over."

"I'm not here for the reception. I'm here to read the will. I'm Mr. and Mrs. Nelson's lawyer."

"We can use my grandfather's study," Trevor said from behind me.

I spun around to see him and Kevin standing there.

The four of us went into the study and sat down.

"I'm sorry to do this today, but it's what your grandfather and grandmother requested," Mr. Randolph said.

Kevin rubbed his hands together in nervousness. "Might as well get this over with."

The lawyer opened his briefcase, pulled out a stack of papers, and handed a packet to each brother. "As you can see, the house, the vehicles, and all the possessions within the home are to be split fifty-fifty among both of you. And below that..." Mr. Randolph cleared his throat. "I apologize. These kinds of stipulations in wills never sit right with me. As I was saying, below that, it discusses Nelson Pharmacy."

Trevor looked at me, eyes wide with uneasiness. I could understand his anxiousness, but the way he'd spoken with Vernon earlier made it clear that he should be the one to take over the family business.

"Are either of you pharmacists?"

"No," both men answered.

Mr. Randolph pulled at the tie around his neck. "Are either of you married?" he asked, glancing at me and the wedding rings on my and Trevor's fingers.

"I am," Trevor said.

The attorney looked at Kevin, who was to his left. "I apologize." He turned back to the three of us. "With that, Nelson Pharmacy is to be inherited by Trevor Nelson."

And just like that, the reason Trevor and I had gotten married was gone.

Chapter Thirty-One

TREVOR

ALEXIS KNOCKED on the door to my office. "I'm just letting you know I'm home."

I looked up from the paperwork in front of me.

She had a wary smile on her face. The last few days, she'd been walking around like she was waiting for something bad to happen.

I pushed my chair away from my desk. "Come over here."

She stepped into the room, and when she was close enough, I grabbed her hand and pulled her over to me, between my legs.

"I'm sorry I haven't paid us much attention lately. I've been so busy with the funeral and now the pharmacy."

"It's fine. I know you have a lot on your plate," she said, and I could tell she meant it, but something was still bothering her.

"Are you sure?"

"Yes."

"Okay, because I'm going to need to leave town in a couple days."

"Why?"

"So, my brother wasn't wrong about the pharmacy making less money than it used to. It had definitely been a good investment when my grandparents opened it."

"Oh, you mean, back when a man with a stay-at-home wife and six kids could live off minimum wage?"

"Uh...yeah."

She'd made a good point.

"The money netted each year is getting smaller and smaller, and soon, it's going to cost more to keep it open than the pharmacy makes."

"It doesn't surprise me that things have changed."

"One of those things is pharmacy brokers, and after doing some research, I found small, independent pharmacies simply can't compete with chain stores."

"What does that mean?"

"It means that I might have to sell Nelson Pharmacy after all, but instead of selling it to some developer who's going to close it and tear it down, I can sell it to a different pharmacy." It sounded like the perfect plan on paper, but there were definite flaws. "The downside: while most employees will probably be able to stay employed, it'll be like starting over. They'll have to interview, and they might not get a job." Saying it out loud sounded depressing. I fell against the back of my chair and rubbed my hands over my face. "I wish things were different."

Alexis leaned over, putting her hands on the arms of my chair. "Hey, you are doing the best you can. I know it sucks, but you are making do with the circumstances of reality. You could give up and tear the place down, but you're trying to save jobs and health care in that area."

I grinned at her. "Thank you."

"You're welcome, but I didn't do much."

I cupped the back of her head. "I'm going to take you to bed now."

———

ALEXIS

I lay next to Trevor with my hand on his chest. The steady beat of his heart thumped under my palm as he rested in bed, and I wanted to memorize this moment forever.

I knew our time together was coming to an end. I had my money, and Trevor had his pharmacy. And now that he didn't have to fight Kevin in court, there was no reason for us to be together. No financial reason anyway.

Every day I came home, part of me expected Trevor to tell me it was time to move out, and the rest of me hoped he'd ask me to stay. But he hadn't said anything so far, and I hadn't wanted to add any more stress to his plate.

But now that he was going out of town, I thought maybe it was a good time.

"When are you leaving?" I asked.

"Two days from now."

While Trevor's heart was slowly beating, my own began to speed up. Fear of rejection was the worst.

"So, I was thinking..."

He lifted an eyelid and peeked at me. "Oh? About what?" he said with a coy smile.

I chuckled. "Not about sex."

"What nonsexual thing were you thinking about?"

I rolled onto my back. I couldn't look at him when I told him my idea.

"I was thinking, when you get back from your trip, we should start dating for real." I'd deliberately chosen confident wording to let him know I was serious. And I was about to tell him all the reasons we should give a real relationship a try.

But a bubble of laughter came out of him before I could speak.

I quickly looked at him, but I wished I hadn't because he started laughing harder.

"Oh, Alexis, that's a good one."

He thought it was funny.

My heart shattered into pieces, and my pride crumbled to dust.

I tried to come up with a witty response, as if I didn't care, like, *I didn't know dating me would be that horrible*, but when I opened my mouth, nothing came out.

I didn't think Trevor would purposely be cruel, and I quickly realized he must have no clue how I felt about him. But maybe I should have known that since he never figured out I'd liked him all those years ago when we met.

I turned away from him on the bed and willed myself not to cry. Because Trevor wasn't a bad guy. If I burst into tears, he'd probably feel awful and change his mind about dating me just to make me feel better.

Unlike some people, I didn't want to be with someone who didn't want to be with me.

Trevor put his arm around me. "Hey, are you okay?"

My stomach rumbled at that moment, and if I could have kissed it, I would have.

"I haven't eaten since lunch. I was thinking about dinner, is all."

"How about we order pizza?"

"Sure."

He kissed me on the cheek and got out of bed. "I'll go put an order in."

"Okay."

After he left, I closed my eyes and counted to ten.

I'd had a marriage end before. I could handle this. I needed to make a game plan, was all. I could do this.

But I needed to do something else first.

I pushed back the covers, got dressed, and headed for the kitchen. Once there, I pulled out ingredients and other items from the fridge, the pantry, and the cupboards.

"Pizza's on its way," Trevor said when he walked in. "What's going on here?" he asked, scanning the counter.

"I'm going to try to make cheesecake."

"Ooh, what's the occasion?"

"I'm thinking of adding it to the menu at The Purrfect Café." That was what I told him anyway, and maybe it would end up being true.

But what I was really thinking was that baking had gotten me through my divorce from Kevin, and it would get me through my heartbreak with Trevor too. At least I had money this time. But while the financial security felt good, it wouldn't mend my broken heart.

Two days later, after he left town, I packed up what few things I had and moved out.

Chapter Thirty-Two

TREVOR

I GOT HOME after being gone for five days, feeling good about the decisions I was about to make. It wasn't perfect, but it was the best choice I could make in a difficult situation. I was making the right decision for everyone involved.

It was late in the day, and I walked into a dark house. Alexis must not have come home from work yet. But it seemed like more than her presence was missing. When I looked around, I found a box of cupcakes and her wedding ring along with a note on the counter.

DEAR TREVOR,
THANK YOU FOR EVERYTHING. I KNOW YOU GOT YOUR INHERITANCE OUT OF THIS MARRIAGE, BUT I CAN NEVER TRULY REPAY YOU FOR GETTING THE MONEY THAT WAS OWED TO ME.

Many people have asked what I'm going to do with it, and first things first. I'm going to get a house. No more crappy apartments for me. And I have you to thank.

I hope everything works out with the pharmacy. Whatever you do, I'm sure you will make the right choice.

I didn't know how we should go about doing the divorce, so if you need me, I'll be at my parents' for now.

All my thanks,

Alexis

I put the letter down before picking it up and reading it again. Then, I flew up the stairs to look in the guest room.

Her things were all gone. No wonder my house felt empty.

I ran back downstairs, grabbed my keys and her ring, and bolted for my car.

———

I made it to Alexis's parents' house as fast as I could. And when her father answered the door, I waited for him to punch me in the face.

I must have had some kind of expression on my face that told him I was waiting for him to hit me because he said, "Alexis explained everything. Thank you for getting that money for her future."

"Oh. It's the least I could do. Is Alexis here?"

"Come in. I'll get her for you."

I waited by the front door as Pat went to look for his daughter.

"Alexis, Trevor's here."

"What?"

"Trevor's here." Pat walked back into the living room with keys in his hand. "She'll be out in a minute."

"Thank you," I said as he headed out the front door.

"Mom, can you tell him I'm not here?"

"Your father already let him know you were."

"Then, tell him I'm sick." She faked a cough, and I wondered if they knew I could hear everything they said.

But more than that, I wondered why Alexis didn't want to talk to me.

"Honey, you're going to have to talk to him."

"I know. I wasn't expecting it to be today though. I thought he'd wait a few weeks, after he had the divorce papers. I was hoping I'd have a few weeks to stop thinking about him."

"Oh, honey."

"I'm so stupid, Mom. I fell in love with him."

"I'm not surprised. Trevor was the one you liked in the first place. Kevin was a consolation prize."

I took a step back and hit the door behind me. I'd had no idea Alexis had liked me back in the day.

"A horrible one at that."

Angie laughed at her daughter's joke. "Okay, but how do you know Trevor doesn't feel the same?"

"I don't want to tell you."

"You know I'll never judge you."

"I know, but it's embarrassing. I put out the idea that we start dating, and he laughed in my face. I know he thought I was joking, but, *oof*, that one hurt."

"Oh, Alexis, I'm sorry."

"It's not your fault, Mom, but thank you. And now that you know, will you please tell him I'm sick?"

"No."

"*Mom.*"

"Honey, the longer you wait to face him, the harder it's going to be. Just go out there and see what he wants. Rip the bandage off. If you need me, I'll be right here."

I was still in shock over the news that Alexis had liked me all those years ago that I almost missed the fake smile she had plastered on her face.

"Hi, Trevor. My dad said you wanted to see me."

When she reached me, I grabbed her wrist and yanked her close.

"I have a question, and I want the truth."

She looked up at me and swallowed. "Okay."

"Years ago, when we met, you liked me?"

She rolled her eyes. "Really?"

"I want the truth."

"Jeez. Okay. Yes, I did. But Kevin told me you didn't like me back, so I left you alone."

"That asshole."

"Why? What did he do?"

I grabbed ahold of Alexis's face and kissed her. "I liked you too. And I like you now. I love you now. This marriage hasn't been fake for me for a long time."

"Why did you laugh at me then?" she whispered.

"Because I thought you were making a joke. Who wants to go backward to dating when we're already happily married?"

"When you put it like that, it makes perfect sense."

I pulled her wedding ring from my pocket and got down on one knee. "Alexis, will you make me the happiest man in the world and continue to be my wife?"

"Say yes," her mom shouted from the other room, where she was peeking around the corner.

Alexis laughed. "Yes."

I stood, picked her up in my arms, and kissed her.

Epilogue

ALEXIS

"ALEXIS, ARE YOU OKAY?" Bree asked.

It was our monthly friends' dinner, and I looked up as everyone stared at me.

"What do you mean?"

"You love that pasta, but you've barely touched it," Bree said.

"Oh. Yeah, I'm fine. It doesn't sound good tonight for some reason. I shouldn't have ordered it."

"Order something else," Paisley suggested.

"Nah. Nothing really sounds good."

"She's been like this all week," Tessa said. "She hasn't touched a chocolate cupcake. The good thing is, our inventory has doubled."

"Ha-ha. I don't eat that many."

Pru smacked her lips together. "I hate to point out the obvious here, but are you and Trevor using protection?"

Isabelle had just taken a bite of food and almost choked on it.

After I made sure our friend could breathe, I looked at Pru. "Weird question to ask, but no."

"And after everything that happened with Kevin and Candace, you didn't want to rethink that?"

"What are you—"

Tessa gasped. "Oh my God. You're pregnant."

"I can't get pregnant. Besides, I just brought a cat home from the café. I'm okay with only having fur babies." I had Trevor now.

"You couldn't get pregnant with Kevin," Pru said. "And now that you know he didn't get Candace pregnant, there is a chance that he was the problem."

A part of me wanted to believe them, but I couldn't let myself.

Elizabeth jumped up from the table. "I'll go buy a test." And before I could stop her, she was hurrying out the front door.

"I think you all are imagining things," I told them as we waited.

"I think Pru's right," Bree said.

I looked around for someone to be on my side, but no one looked like they were going to agree with me.

Elizabeth was back in ten minutes and shoved the bag at me. "Take it now."

"No," I said with a laugh but stopped when six sets of

serious eyes looked back at me. "Okay, fine, I'll go take a test."

I went to the bathroom, pulled out a test, and read the directions. I managed to get it done without peeing on my hand, but I wasn't sure what to do with it for the next three minutes.

Turned out, nothing. The plus sign turned pink as soon as my urine traveled down the stick.

Holy fucking shit, I'm pregnant.

I walked back to the table in a daze and sat down with a thump.

Pru looked at her watch. "You're done already?"

"It's positive."

My friends started clapping and giving me hugs.

Tessa grinned at me. "You'd better call Trevor."

I grinned back, still in awe. "I think I'm going to wait until I get home." I wanted to see his face.

But I did pick up my phone and text him.

Me: I have a surprise for you when I get home.

Trevor: Dessert?

Me: Something better.

Trevor: You?

Me: Something even better than that.

Trevor: Nothing's better than you.

I smiled. I so loved this man.

Me: I guess we'll find out when I get home.

"Sebastian," Bree shouted.

I raised my head to see her waving her arm to someone across the room, and when I looked over, I saw her cousin walking over.

"Hey, coz," Bree said, giving him a hug. "What are you doing here?"

"Getting some dinner with a couple of guys from work." Sebastian looked around. "Good evening, ladies."

We all smiled and said hello because how could we not? Sebastian was tall, dark, and handsome.

Except for Pru. She gave a single wave and looked away.

"You're with colleagues. Are you here on business or pleasure?" Bree asked.

"A little bit of both. I'm the new guy at work, so everyone nominated me to plan the annual charity event." He smiled a fake smile. "Aren't I a lucky guy?"

"Oh my God," Bree said. "Pru is an event planner. I bet she'd give you the friends and family discount."

Pru jumped off her chair. "No, I will not."

Sebastian eyed Pru and smiled. "Sounds like a plan."

"Did you hear me? I already said no."

"Come on, Pru. It's a charity event," Bree said.

"Yeah, Pru," Paisley agreed.

"I don't even know what the event is."

"It's the Annual Golden Prairie Firefighters Charity Event. This year, we're giving the proceeds away to..." He winced. "I'll have to get back to you on that one."

"I've been to this event, Pru," I said. "They always pick excellent charities." In the past, I had gone with Kevin, but maybe this year, I could go with my new husband.

Pru put her hands on her hips. "Are you saying you're a firefighter?"

Sebastian held out his arms. "Guilty."

"I don't believe you."

He laughed in disbelief. "Bree?"

She frowned at Pru. "He's always been a fireman."

Pru sat down and crossed her arms and legs. "I'm not doing it."

"Yes, she is," Bree told Sebastian. "I'll make sure she gets your contact info."

After Sebastian left to join his coworkers, Bree looked at Pru. "Why won't you do this? I bet this thing would be a walk in the park for you."

"Because I don't want to, okay?"

I studied Pru, and I didn't know if pregnancy made me more intuitive or what, but I figured out the reason she didn't want to do it.

Pru was attracted to Sebastian, but boy, did she not want to be.

I started laughing.

Another one bites the dust.

Author Note: To find out what happens when Alexis gets home, keep reading in *Not Another Alpha Male*.

Turn the page for a sample of

NOT ANOTHER ALPHA MALE

Not Another Alpha Male

PRU

"Pru."

Sighing, I turned around to see that Sebastian had followed me outside the restaurant. His dark hair blew in the wind, and his brown eyes were locked on me.

I sighed. "What?"

He waved my card between his first two fingers. "I can't come to your office tomorrow at nine," he said when he reached me.

I smiled and shrugged. "Oh well. At least I tried." As I spun on my heel, my smile turned to a grin.

Until Sebastian grabbed my hand and twirled me back around. I almost bumped into him but just managed to stop short.

He clenched his jaw. "Tomorrow is Thursday. You know, most people have to work on Thursdays. You're doing this on purpose."

This close to him, I could tell how good he smelled. It made me think of getting naked.

"Pru."

Oh. I turned my head away and took a deep breath of non-Sebastian air. "Fine. Do you think you could call me at nine instead?"

He nodded. "Yes."

Dammit.

"Okay, we'll talk at nine then."

This time, when I walked away, he let me go. I hoped sometime between now and nine tomorrow morning, he'd magically lose my card.

I picked up fast food on the way home since I had left my friends before eating dinner. Then, I went home and sat in front of the TV while I ate dinner. I loved my friends, but I didn't mind a quiet night alone.

After I calmed down, I picked up my phone and texted my friends.

> Me: I'm sorry I overreacted and left the restaurant.

> Bree: Who is this?

> Tessa: Yeah, I don't recognize this number.

Paisley: How did you get on our message thread?

Me: I'm a shitty friend.

Bree: Oh, it's Pru.

She followed it up with a laugh emoji.

Me: I'm glad to see you're not mad.

Isabelle: Nah, we had a long talk after you left. It's okay that you left us.

Me: A long talk? About me? What did you say about me?

Elizabeth: Not about you specifically. Just about life.

Me: I don't believe a word of that.

Isabelle: LOL. But you have no choice.

Me: Hey, where's Alexis?

Paisley: She went home to tell Trevor she's pregnant. They're probably doing it right now.

Elizabeth: How is finding out you're pregnant sexy?

I shook my head and smiled. I wished Elizabeth would just be true to herself and the rest of us. No one would judge her.

> Paisley: How can it not be?

I didn't really get how my friends could be so clueless. Elizabeth didn't look at a guy and think, *Put a baby in me*, or, *He's so hot that my ovaries exploded.* That was why she didn't understand the concept.

Unlike everyone else, I was going to have mercy on Elizabeth.

> Me: First of all, it depends on the person. Obviously, people can be ecstatic, and others can panic. And some don't want to have sex with their partner.

> Me: But there is something about knowing this hot guy that you love put a baby in you. It's like a primal thing. He's marked you forever.

> Bree: Pru, I had no idea.

> Paisley: Pru has a breeding kink.

> Me: No, I don't. BUT I can understand how people do. And I don't judge.

> Bree: Ha! You judge Sebastian, and you hardly know him.

That was because he was the kind of guy women wanted to put babies in them. Just because he was good-looking and walked around like he had a big dick.

Alexis: I'm here! And, no, I wasn't having sex. But I do have something to share with you.

Saved by Alexis.

I didn't want to justify my animosity toward Sebastian. A few months ago, Bree would have understood, but now, she was engaged to a former manwhore. She wouldn't get it.

The next message that came across my phone was a video from Alexis. As I hit play, I scooted down on my couch as if I were going to watch a movie or something.

The clip started with Alexis outside her door and her walking into her house. We couldn't see her, but she was obviously the one recording.

I watched as she walked into the living room, where her husband, Trevor, was lounging on the couch with a bag of chips and a cat on his lap. His eyes lit up when he saw Alexis, and my breath caught at the love in his eyes.

"How was dinner?" His gaze shifted to her hand, and he grinned. "Are those leftovers for me?"

"You can have them. I wasn't very hungry."

Trevor frowned as he moved the cat from his legs and stood. "Are you feeling okay?" he asked, taking the box of food from her and leaning forward. He disappeared from the camera as the sound of a kiss was picked up by the microphone.

They both headed for the kitchen, and the image on

the camera got shaky until I realized that Alexis was propping up her phone, so she could record the two of them together.

Trevor sat at the counter and lifted the lid on the to-go box while Alexis pulled open a drawer and handed him a fork.

"Remember how I said I have a surprise for you?"

"How could I forget? That was only a few hours ago." He stabbed a piece of food and popped it into his mouth. "Are you doing something with The Purrfect Café?"

"I can see why you'd guess that, but no." Alexis smiled as she bit her lip with nervousness and reached into her pocket. She pulled out her pregnancy test and slid it over to Trevor.

His brow furrowed in confusion as he picked it up and studied it.

I could tell when he realized what he was looking at, and I almost started crying.

The expression on his face was priceless.

He slowly raised his eyes up to his wife. "Is this what I think it is?"

Alexis had already given in to her emotions and had tears flowing down her cheeks. She nodded and stepped away from the counter.

Trevor jumped out of his seat and scooped her up into his arms. She clung to him in a way that showed she loved and trusted him.

I didn't think I had ever experienced that with any man I'd ever dated.

"How did this happen?" Trevor asked when he set her down on her feet.

"Since Kevin didn't actually get Candace pregnant and my fertility studies came back fine, it was probably him that whole time we were married and trying. I hope that means you're okay with this."

Trevor cupped her face. "Alexis Nelson, I'm ecstatic."

That was where the video cut off, and I put my phone down with a sigh.

I was so happy for my friend—I was happy for all my friends—but there was a twinge of jealousy in my chest. I knew I was better off alone, but sometimes, it still hurt anyway.

About the Author

R.L. Kenderson is two best friends writing under one name.

Renae has always loved reading, and in third grade, she wrote her first poem where she learned she might have a knack for this writing thing. Lara remembers sneaking her grandmother's Harlequin novels when she was probably too young to be reading them, and since then, she knew she wanted to write her own.

When they met in college, they bonded over their love of reading and the TV show *Charmed*. What really spiced up their friendship was when Lara introduced Renae to romance novels. When they discovered their first vampire romance, they knew there would always be a special place in their hearts for paranormal romance. After being unable to find certain storylines and characteristics they wanted to read about in the hundreds of books they consumed, they decided to write their own.

One lives in the Minneapolis-St. Paul area and the other in the Kansas City area where they both work in the medical field during the day and a sexy author by night.

They communicate through phone, email, and whole lot of messaging.

You can find them at http://www.rlkenderson.com, Facebook, Instagram, TikTok, and Goodreads. Join their reader group! Or you can email them at rlkenderson@ rlkenderson.com, or sign up for their newsletter. They always love hearing from their readers.